DOCTOR WHO AND THE ENEMY OF THE WORLD

Based on the BBC television serial by David Whitaker by arrangement with the British Broadcasting Corporation

IAN MARTER

A TARGET BOOK
published by
the paperback division of
W. H. ALLEN & Co. Ltd

A Target Book
Published in 1981
by the Paperback Division of W. H. Allen & Co. Ltd
A Howard & Wyndham Company
44 Hill Street W1X 8LB

Reprinted 1982

Printed in Great Britain by
The Anchor Press Ltd, Tiptree, Essex

ISBN 0 426 20126 4

Contents

1	A Day by the Sea	7
2	The Doctor Takes a Risk	19
3	Volcanoes	31
4	Too Many Cooks	45
5	Seeds of Suspicion	56
6	The Secret Empire	70
7	A Scrap of Truth	84
8	Deceptions	95
9	Unexpected Evidence	108
10	The Doctor Not Himself	119

1

A Day by the Sea

The hot January sun beat out of the cloudless blue sky and a warm northeast wind blew the Coral Sea into a roaring froth over the Great Barrier Reef. The Australian summer was at its height. Between the tangle of thick vegetation covering the dunes and the crashing cascades of breaking waves, a broad beach of fine white sand wobbled in the relentless heat. There was no sign of life except for something moving swiftly over the clear water about two kilometres from the shore, enveloped in a curtain of shimmering spray. On land the only movement was the ceaseless rustling of dense tropical foliage and the zigzagging swarms of huge sandflies buzzing angrily over the sparkling sand in search of prey.

Suddenly, above the distant thundering of the reef, there came an unearthly grinding and howling sound—as if ancient and rusted machinery were being forced back into life. Up near the dunes a small section of beach about two metres square suddenly sank slightly, as if under the weight of some invisible object. The shriek of tortured machinery grew to a shrill climax and a faint yellow light began to blink above the rectangular hollow. Then, as abruptly as it had begun, the hideous noise ceased, the yellow light went out and the sand settled. When the air had cleared, a scruffy blue police box stood listing drunkenly on the sloping beach. Finally, with a sharp crack, it lurched back onto an even keel and there was silence.

Then a babble of excited voices erupted inside. The door swung open and a stocky young lad with straight dark hair and rugged features stepped warily out, blinking in the fierce sunlight. His keen eyes rapidly scanned the vast expanse of shimmering sand.

'And where have you landed us this time Doctor?' he called, relaxing a little.

'We're at the seaside of course, stupid!' retorted a rather cultured female voice. A pale, pretty young lady wearing a faded Victorian dress emerged from the police box behind him, shading her large blue eyes from the glare.

'Aye I ken that right enough, Miss Victoria, but *where*?' the sturdy young Highlander replied with a scowl.

'How on earth should I know, Jamie?' she said. 'Where *are* we, Doctor?' she cried, peering into the darkened doorway.

Seconds later a dapper figure clad in a worn, black velvet jacket and baggy check trousers darted out into the sunlight.

'Oh, do stop fussing you two. Go and find some buckets and spades in the TARDIS and let's enjoy ourselves,' the little man urged them, looking expectantly around him. He strode eagerly off towards the sea, loosening his spotted necktie and then waving his arms about as he took deep lungfuls of fresh air.

The young Scot stared after him. 'Buckets and spades! Is he after digging for worms?' he muttered.

Victoria had reached into the police box and was putting on a wide-brimmed straw hat. 'Don't be silly, Jamie. He wants us to help him build a sandcastle,' she giggled, skipping after the Doctor.

James Robert McCrimmon looked incredulously around him. 'Sandcastles ...' he muttered. His scowling face glistening with sweat, he marched down the beach to join the Doctor and Victoria at the water's edge.

Having removed his shoes and socks and rolled up his trousers, the Doctor was splashing his feet in the shallows and chuckling with delight. 'This is marvellous, marvellous,' he cried, starting to dance a sort of jig. 'You two don't know what you're missing.'

Jamie stood motionless and open-mouthed, staring out to sea. 'Whatever's the matter, Jamie?' Victoria asked, following his gaze.

She watched something skimming rapidly across the surface between the reef and the shore, throwing up great showers of rainbow spray. Then her ears picked up a high-pitched whining above the crashing surf. Suddenly afraid, she clutched the Doctor's arm. 'Look, Doctor,' she murmured, 'whatever is it?'

Aboard the hovercraft a thickset gray-haired man was examining the three distant figures on the beach through powerful binoculars. He snapped an order to the muscular young man beside him at the controls. 'Hey, Rod, pull 'er up a second.'

'What's up then, Tony?'

'There's some crazy nutter dancing a jig out there,' the older man growled in a thick Australian accent. 'I don't believe it. It can't be. No way ...'

'What the hell's eating you?' Rod exclaimed, grabbing the binoculars and peering at the tiny figure hopping about on the shore. 'Jeez ...' he gasped a moment later: What's *he* doing here?' He padded across the deck and thrust the binoculars into the hands of a tall thin man wearing a crumpled suit, who was sitting reading a tattered magazine. 'Just take a look at this, Tibor,' he said, grabbing the man by the lapels and yanking him bodily to his feet. 'Over there in the water.'

The thin man trained the glasses on the shore in the middle of the bay. 'It is not possible, Tony,' he said in a harsh Teutonic accent, without looking round. 'It's quite impossible,' he told them, lowering the glasses and turning to face them. 'But there is no doubt at all. It is Salamander himself.'

There was a stunned silence.

'So. What we gonna do then, Tony?' Rod blurted out at last.

The gray-haired man whipped a small walkie-talkie out of his belt. 'What do ya think, dumbo?' he drawled with a scornful grin, and he pressed the switch.

About ten kilometres inland in a town called Melville on a hill overlooking the ocean, a tall attractive woman of thirty was standing in front of a large wall map hanging in a spacious office, situated in a deserted concrete and glass building. A small radio clipped to her belt suddenly gave a shrill bleep. With an impatient toss of her head she unclipped it and snapped the switch without taking her eyes from the map. 'Astrid,' she said coldly.

'This is Tony,' crackled the receiver, 'we're between Cape Melville and Heath Point. We've caught the Big One.'

For a moment the young woman said nothing. She stared at the map, her mind racing. 'That's impossible,' she retorted at last, 'he's just gone off to the Central European Zone. You must be mistaken.'

Out on the hovercraft Tony thumped the chart table impatiently. 'I tell you it's Salamander. Not a shadow of a doubt,' he shouted into his radio. 'The three of us have all had a good look at him.'

There was a long pause. Eventually Astrid replied. 'All right, Tony. If you are quite certain, I will inform Giles and ...'

Tony snatched up the binoculars with his free hand and swept the horizon. 'No way. We'll handle this by ourselves,' he said savagely.

Astrid's voice crackled urgently from the receiver. 'You will wait for instructions from Giles,' she cried. 'There must be no mistakes.'

But no one aboard the hovercraft was listening any longer. Tony flung down the radio and punched Rod's enormous arm. 'Let's move, Rod,' he snapped.

While Tony kept watch on the distant figures of the Doctor and his two companions, Tibor took down from a rack three high-velocity rifles equipped with telescopic sights and laid them on the chart table. His hands shaking with excitement, he checked each weapon with expert thoroughness, his thin lips curled in a vicious smile.

In Giles Kent's office Astrid was talking intensely to a man facing her from the small screen of a videophone installed on top of the stainless-steel desk.

'Giles, they're convinced that it's Salamander and they intend to kill him,' she explained.

Giles Kent leaned forward, knotted veins standing out on his bony temples. 'They're just a bunch of cowboys,' he snorted. 'We can't afford any mistakes now, Astrid, you understand? You must stop them,' he said icily. 'Get out there at once and stop them.' The screen went blank.

Meanwhile, on the beach, the Doctor was attempting to explain the principle of the hovercraft to his two young friends.

'It's like some kind of sea monster,' Victoria murmured, unable to take her eyes from the swiftly approaching craft.

The Doctor chuckled indulgently. 'Well, my dear, it looks as if you'll be able to examine it at close quarters in a minute.'

At that moment something zipped through the air. Victoria's straw hat was whipped off her head and sent spinning across the sand.

Jamie stared at the startled girl. 'What the divil…' His voice died as something whined into the sand by the Doctor's foot.

For a moment no one moved. 'Run!' the Doctor yelled, suddenly wheeling round and scampering off up the beach bent almost double.

They heard the hovercraft's engines shrieking closer and closer behind them as it approached land and bullets tore relentlessly into the sand all around them. They flung themselves into a hollow in the dunes, gasping for breath and soaked in sweat.

'We must try to reach the TARDIS,' the Doctor shouted. But the hovercraft was already slithering up onto the beach, its huge propellors whipping the sand into the air. In a few seconds it would be between them and the police box. 'It's no good. We'll have to get round through the trees,' the Doctor cried, plunging into the dense undergrowth. As Jamie and Victoria fought their way after him they heard the engines fading as the hovercraft settled on the sand and the three men jumped down and spread out in pursuit.

Crouching low, Jamie dragged Victoria up a steep

slope where the vegetation was less thickly tangled. Straight ahead of them the huge figure of Rod suddenly loomed up and took aim at the Doctor's retreating back. Jamie charged like a young bull and butted Rod in the stomach, catching the top-heavy muscleman off balance and sending him crashing against an exposed rock, which he hit with the side of his head. Rod lay quite still.

'Bull's-eye, Jamie!' Victoria cheered. Clutching his throbbing head, Jamie staggered over and urged her forward.

The Doctor had seen Tibor and Tony closing in on them along the beach, their rifles glinting in the sun. Jamie and Victoria almost fell on top of him as they scrambled down into a hollow where he was waiting for them, concealed in some huge leaves.

At that moment a hail of bullets tore through the foliage around them as Tony and Tibor fired at random into the bushes.

There followed a menacing silence while the two men from the hovercraft slowly circled round the area where their quarry were hidden. Suddenly Tony stopped dead and listened intently. A steady throbbing sound was coming rapidly closer. 'What the hell's that?' he snarled. Tony screwed up his eyes against the glare. They watched as the helicopter made a wide turn high above the hovercraft and then banked over the inland edge of the dunes and hung in the air. 'It's Astrid!' Tony yelled furiously. 'Come on, let's finish the job quick.'

Slapping fresh magazines into their guns, they ploughed into the tangled thickets, determined to find their man and kill him.

The Doctor stood up cautiously and the helicopter

turned and glided down until it was almost on top of them. 'What is it, Doctor?' Jamie shouted, his hands clasped tightly over his ears.

At that moment the cockpit door opened and Astrid leaned out. 'Come on, run for it,' she screamed at the three figures huddled below.

The Doctor stared up at the strange young woman for a few seconds. Then he grabbed his companions and started to drag them towards the helicopter. The Doctor pushed Jamie into the cockpit after Victoria and then clambered up and squeezed himself into the tiny space beside them. With a surge of power the helicopter rose swiftly at a steep angle. A hail of bullets ricocheted off the fuselage as Astrid swung the machine violently to and fro in an attempt to confuse their attackers.

'A very timely and welcome rescue, dear lady,' the Doctor shouted across to Astrid. He put a comforting hand on Victoria's shoulder. 'Well, at least we're safe now,' he yelled with a grin.

But the grin soon vanished as he frowned at the instrument panel in front of them. 'You're losing fuel very quickly, my dear,' he shouted across to Astrid.

She glanced down. 'They must have got the tank,' she yelled back, making a turn and flying directly away from the sea.

The Doctor twisted round and squinted through the rear of the cockpit. Liquid was streaming out of several holes in the fuel tank behind them. 'We could explode at any moment ...' he breathed.

Less than a minute later Astrid let the helicopter drop like a stone, then slowed the dizzying descent at the last moment to land on a concrete pad next to a long low bungalow set in a grove of luxuriant trees and shrubs a few hundred metres from the sea. As she led the way quickly into the cool ultramodern building, she suddenly swayed and would have stumbled if the Doctor had not caught her.

'Wait, my dear ... you're hurt,' he said anxiously.

She tried to pull her arm away. 'It's just a scratch,' she said. 'We're lucky to be alive.'

Despite her insistance that she was all right, the Doctor made her sit down in the spacious living room and sent his two friends to find a medical kit.

Astrid stared closely at the Doctor as he perched on the arm of her chair and carefully rolled back the ripped sleeve, trying to ignore the young woman's searching gaze.

'Just who on earth *are* you?' she asked eventually, leaning back and studying him as if he were some extraordinary exhibit in a museum.

The Doctor looked surprised. 'I thought perhaps you knew. You risked your life to save us.'

Jamie followed Victoria back into the room. 'Don't you worry yourself, lassie. The Doctor will fix you up just fine,' he told Astrid with a smile, as Victoria handed the Doctor a small first-aid pack they had found.

Astrid watched the Doctor examine the label on a tiny aerosol spray. 'You are a doctor?' she said doubtfully.

The Doctor looked a little taken aback. 'I am The Doctor,' he replied emphatically, 'but I fear medicine is not my speciality.'

'You're being evasive,' she protested angrily. She winced as the stranger began to bind her arm with polygauze bandage.

The Doctor looked up innocently. 'And what about

you?' he inquired. 'Who are you?'

'My name is Astrid Ferrier.'

The Doctor bowed slightly and introduced Victoria and Jamie. Then he rolled the sleeve down over the rather crooked lumpy dressing. 'There, that should do it,' he grinned.

Astrid shook her head slowly. 'It's not possible,' she murmured, still gazing at the Doctor. 'No wonder they're so determined to kill you.'

The Doctor frowned. 'Oh yes, I had almost forgotten our friends in the hovercraft. Why are they so anxious to kill us?'

'Kill *you*,' Astrid corrected him sharply. 'They hate you.'

'But I am the nicest and most inoffensive creature in the entire universe.' The Doctor glanced up reproachfully at Victoria and Jamie. 'Really this planet of yours is the most hostile and irrational place I have ever known,' he complained.

Astrid put her hand on his arm. 'I meant that they hate who they *think* you are. They will stop at nothing to destroy you.'

Victoria looked shocked. 'Well, can't you make them see their mistake?' she chimed in. 'Surely *you* don't hate the Doctor?'

Astrid smiled for the first time since they had met her. 'Quite the contrary. To me the Doctor is the most precious person ever to drop from the skies.'

The Doctor beamed with modest pleasure. 'I fear you do less than justice to your considerable skill as a pilot, Miss Ferrier,' he joked.

Astrid's smile vanished as unexpectedly as it had appeared. 'I rescued you because I want you to help me,' she said. 'You are almost the exact double of a man who

16

will stop at nothing to achieve total mastery over the entire world. He must be stopped at all costs.'

There was an awkward silence.

'Who?' Jamie exclaimed.

'Salamander,' Astrid said. The word seemed to hang in the air like a threat. Astrid walked over and stood face to face with the Doctor. 'I have no idea who you are or where you come from, but it is quite possible that you can save the world,' she said earnestly. 'Please will you help us? There is very little time.'

There was a long silence while the Doctor ruffled his hair, examined his fingernails, whistled a few bars of a catchy tune under his breath, raised his eyebrows and clicked his teeth. Then he looked at Astrid and a strange expression came into his eyes.

As soon as she saw that look, Victoria clutched at his arm. 'Doctor, you're not going to accept ... are you?' she pleaded hopelessly.

The next moment all hell seemed to break loose. The fading whine of a hovercraft's turbines suddenly penetrated the bungalow on the gusting wind and an instant later there was a ferocious battering on the door.

Astrid moved with the speed and agility of a cat. 'Quick, the terrace,' she whispered. But even as she reached the glass patio doors Tibor appeared, rifle at the ready, on the paved terrace at the back of the bungalow. She ran back and slipped behind the arch dividing the long L-shaped room. The Doctor had already pulled Jamie and Victoria down behind a large couch.

Tibor shot the locks out of the patio door and slid it open. Warily he entered the room. As he reached the arch, Astrid grabbed his arm with her good hand and threw him expertly over her shoulder. Jamie broke cover and seized the rifle as Tibor hit the floor. Then, with Victoria and the

17

Doctor close on his heels, he dashed after Astrid. As they rushed out onto the terrace, the main door was punched off its hinges and Rod lumbered in, firing wildly at the staggering figure silhouetted in the middle of the room. Tibor was thrown back against the thick glass of the terrace window by the force of the spraying high-velocity bullets.

As Tibor slumped to the floor, Tony ran in through the front doorway. 'What the hell have you done, you muscle-bound ape?' he yelled at Rod who was staring down at Tibor's body and muttering excuses with tears in his eyes. 'No time now,' Tony shouted, making for the terrace. 'Come on, he's getting away.'

The four fugitives reached the trees at the edge of the grove surrounding the bungalow and froze in the under-growth. They waited, glancing anxiously at one another, scarcely daring to breathe. Then they heard the whine of the helicopter engine starting and a few seconds later it roared up over the bungalow and hovered overhead. A savage storm of gunfire erupted in the sky and bullets strafed the grove from end to end.

Suddenly there was a massive explosion and a vivid orange flash lit up the trees. The blazing wreckage of the helicopter spiralled out of the sky and smashed into the garden below the terrace, followed by a rain of twisted, flaring, metal fragments. A huge pall of thick rubbery smoke belched into the air and hung there like a gigantic black finger pointing to disaster.

2

The Doctor Takes a Risk

An hour later the Doctor, his two friends and Astrid were standing in Giles Kent's office and Giles Kent was studying the Doctor with undisguised astonishment. 'Incredible! It's quite incredible!' he exclaimed at last.

The Doctor cleared his throat uncomfortably. 'I am not a laboratory specimen, Mr Kent,' he protested gently.

Kent apologised profusely and invited the Doctor to sit down. 'But you must surely be aware of the uncanny resemblance yourself,' he said. 'Salamander is a world figure.'

The Doctor rubbed his nose and smiled secretively. 'My companions and I have been ... well, a little out of touch with things lately,' he explained.

Astrid moved impatiently over to the desk. 'Show him the videowire, Giles,' she said. 'We're wasting valuable time.'

Kent took a small cassette from a drawer and inserted it into the video apparatus on his desk. He turned the screen round to face the Doctor and switched on. 'This recording shows Salamander addressing the 13th United Zones Conference on World Resources in Geneva last year,' he explained, as Astrid dimmed the lights.

The Doctor leaned forward and peered intently at the screen. A small figure was seen mounting a dais in the centre of a vast, domed auditorium crowded with row upon row of delegates, all applauding enthusiastically. The picture snapped into close-up. The Doctor's jaw dropped and his eyes widened in amazement. Both Jamie and Victoria gasped at what they saw.

On the screen the Doctor appeared to be acknowledging the delegates' applause and arranging his notes. His hair had been trimmed and slicked back with oil so that it shone, and so that his ears were fully visible. His eyebrows had grown bushier. His eyes were perhaps deeper set and his nose rather longer. His mouth was fuller and his lips slightly curled. His dazzling white shirt was clasped at the throat with an ornamental clip and his dark jacket was familiar except for its short, upright collar. Jamie and Victoria kept glancing from the screen to the Doctor and back again, scarcely able to believe their eyes. The resemblance was fantastic.

Salamander began his speech in a thick South American accent. 'Mr President, I am delighted to report excellent progress with the Conservation Project at Kanowa in the Australasian Zone. I can announce today that the Mark 3 Suncatcher is successfully in orbit and although we cannot yet guarantee beautiful summers for everyone, we can promise to concentrate even more sunlight into deprived zones. I can tell you that at this very moment in the great Siberian plains the wheat is ripening in the sun ...'

At this point the audience broke into spontaneous applause and the screen showed a big close-up of Salamander's face flushed with success as he boasted of his project's achievements. The endless statistics poured out, regularly interrupted by bursts of applause from the delegates. Eventually Kent switched off the video machine and Astrid turned up the lights.

The Doctor continued to stare at the blank screen. 'This Salamander of yours seems to be quite a public benefactor, Kent,' he exclaimed, eventually breaking the long silence. 'Rather handsome too, don't you think?'

'Some poor fools regard him as a saviour, Doctor,' Giles snorted.

The Doctor leaned forward. 'Saviour? From what?' he asked sharply.

'Starvation,' Astrid replied. 'Too many people, too little food...'

'Until Salamander developed the Suncatcher,' Kent went on. 'Using the Suncatcher, Salamander manipulates the climate to grow several crops in the same season and he's even transformed waste areas into fertile farmland.'

Jamie had kept quiet for some time. 'This Salamander's a magician,' he exclaimed suddenly. 'I can't see why anybody wants to kill him if he's saving the world.'

'Salamander is evil. He's power-mad. He plans to take control of the entire World Zones Organisation,' Giles said vehemently.

'Do you have any proof, Kent? Any evidence?' asked the Doctor.

'I was once Deputy Security Commissioner for Europe and North Africa in the WZO. When Salamander discovered I had evidence against him, he had me discredited and I was dismissed.'

'So you could quite simply be out to destroy Salamander to get your revenge,' the Doctor murmured, rubbing his chin. 'No wonder your bully boys were so keen to finish me off this afternoon.'

'They acted against my authority, Doctor. I should have apologised.' Kent sat down and switched on the

21

machine again. A series of still photographs flashed up on the screen. Kent gave a brief commentary on each one as it appeared.

'Mikhail Assevski—Controller Central Asian Zone. Drowned 100 metres off shore in Lake Baikal. Assevski was a former Olympic Marathon-Swim Gold Medallist.

'Lars Helvig—Arctic Zone Deputy. Found dead in his office, supposed suicide but no known reason.

'John Freremont—European Zone Commissioner. Brutally murdered. No arrests were ever made.

'Jean Ferrier—' Here Kent paused and glanced across at Astrid. She was staring out of the window at the gathering darkness. Kent cleared his throat and continued.

'Jean Ferrier—Finance Deputy, European Zone. An expert skier but disappeared, presumed dead, on nursery slopes in perfect weather …'

Kent switched the video machine off. There was a long and heavy silence.

Eventually the Doctor went across to Astrid and laid his hand gently on her shoulder. 'Your father?' he asked softly.

She nodded and then turned to him, her green eyes brimming with tears, which she abruptly brushed away. 'Doctor, all those men had met with Salamander or with his sidekick, Benik, very shortly before their deaths,' she said, putting on a brave face.

'And they were all replaced by stooges, by men known to be in Salamander's pocket,' Kent added.

The Doctor turned to him sharply. 'Known by whom?'

'By me, Doctor.'

'Then why didn't you bring Salamander to justice?' he asked.

Kent thumped the desk in frustration. 'Don't you understand? I'm discredited and Salamander gets more popular every day. Worst of all the WZO security supremo is a man called Donald Bruce and he's convinced I'm out to avenge myself on that repulsive reptile. He watches me like a hawk.'

The Doctor looked doubtful. 'If Salamander's methods are as crude as you suggest, surely other people besides yourself must suspect him. You must have allies, Mr Kent.'

'Oh sure, except that most of them are dead.' Kent began to move agitatedly around the office. 'Now there's really only Alexander Denes, Controller of Central European Zone,' he went on, 'and he's so damned cautious, he's more of a liability than an ally.'

'Well', the Doctor murmured, 'the situation seems to be: do we believe Mr Kent or do we not?'

There was an embarrassing pause.

At last Kent broke the silence. 'There is a way you can find out for yourself, Doctor,' he said. 'Impersonate Salamander and penetrate his organisation.'

'I thought you would never ask me!' exclaimed the Doctor. Thrusting his hands deep into his sagging pockets, he began to walk animatedly up and down. 'But there is a great deal more to it than mere appearance. What about the voice? The problem of phonetics?' He stopped by the windows for a moment, muttering quietly away to himself. Then he turned to face the others, frowning with concentration. 'I can announce today that the Mark 3 Suncatcher is successfully in orbit. I can tell you that in the great Siberian plains the wheat is ripening in the sun,' he said, quoting from Salamander's speech.

Victoria clapped eagerly. Giles Kent and Astrid

Ferrier were obviously astounded at the Doctor's mimicry.

'Yes, yes, I think I've got quite close,' he mused, reverting to his own voice. He turned to Giles. 'I'd say he comes from Mexico—Yucatan or Quintana Roo perhaps?'

Kent seized his arm delightedly. 'Amazing. Salamander was born in Mérida, the state capital of Yucatan,' he cried. 'Doctor, you're a genius.'

The Doctor bowed modestly, clearly pleased with himself. 'I fancy I could get it in time. But suppose I do, Kent. What then?'

Giles led him over to the large wall map. 'Simple, Doctor. You walk into Salamander's Research Centre at Kanowa here, find out what he's up to, and there's your proof. I keep some spare clothes in the other office, Doctor. Fortunately we are about the same size. Would you like to try dressing up for the part?'

Suddenly heavy footsteps and voices were heard out in the lobby. Kent grabbed hold of the Doctor, pushed him into the inner office and closed the door.

At the same instant the outer door flew open and two armed WZO guards crashed into the office and stood flanking the doorway, covering the four startled occupants with streamlined automatic pistols. Close behind them a very large gray-haired man walked slowly into the office, his small rimless spectacles flashing as he took in the scene, a faint humourless smile playing around his fleshy mouth. 'Hallo, Kent. Been doing a wee bit of recruiting, have we?' he remarked in his unexpectedly soft, resonant voice. He surveyed Jamie and Victoria in turn, his tongue prodding his pale cheek. 'Bit young for terrorists, aren't they?' he laughed.

Victoria stepped forward, her chin jutting forward defiantly. 'What do you mean?' she demanded.

'All right, Bruce. To what do we owe this pleasure?' Kent inquired.

Donald Bruce ignored him. 'Identify yourselves!' he rapped at the two outlandishly dressed teenagers.

'James Robert McCrimmon and Miss Victoria Waterfield,' said Jamie, with exaggerated emphasis.

The security supremo studied him for a while, his eyes invisible behind the flashing spectacles. Then he turned abruptly to Astrid. 'That bungalow out in Cedar Distric belongs to you, I believe.'

Astrid nodded but said nothing.

Bruce lumbered heavily over to her. 'No doubt you are here to explain to Mr Kent why three of his employees are lying dead on your property.'

Astrid met Bruce's harsh stare and remained silent.

'You were seen at the bungalow late this afternoon in the company of these two kids and another stranger,' Bruce continued. 'Let's deal with this other man first, shall we?' He snapped his fingers and pointed to the door of the inner office.

One guard stamped across to open it, while the other covered the door with his machine pistol.

Victoria would have cried out with astonishment if Jamie had not quickly given her hand a sharp warning squeeze, for out of the inner office stepped Salamander. 'Good evening, Bruce,' he purred, with a dazzling smile. 'What are you doing here?'

Even in the bright fluorescent lighting the transformation was miraculous. The Doctor had sleeked back his hair and fluffed up his eyebrows. His face seemed longer and his eyes deeper-set than usual. Even his mouth looked thicker-lipped and it curled slightly when he spoke. Kent's plain but smart black jacket fitted perfectly and the Doctor had pinned the fresh white shirt at his throat with an expensive-looking clasp. The Doctor's shabby check trousers had been replaced by dark tapering slacks. But it was the voice which really clinched the effect.

Bruce was completely flabbergasted. His pasty complexion flushed as he tried to recover his composure. 'Good ... good evening, Leader. I was under the impression that you had travelled to the Central European Zone yesterday,' he faltered.

The Doctor nodded. 'You were meant to think so.' Waving the guard aside, he walked into the centre of the office with Salamander's characteristic short strides and upright posture.

Bruce frowned unhappily. 'But Leader, how can I possibly provide security if I am misinformed about your movements?'

'My dear Bruce, you have a policeman's mind,' the Doctor said wearily. 'I am sorry for you.'

Bruce walked heavily across to the Doctor and murmured confidentially into his ear. 'Leader we have always agreed that this man Kent is a bad security risk. You ordered constant surveillance and regular reports on his activities. Now I find you here in his office. I feel I am entitled to some explanation.'

The Doctor gave a loud patronising laugh. 'Of course you shall receive an explanation,' he cried, 'when I return from Europe. For the present I am pursuing some highly confidential matters personally, is that clear? I shall see you on my return from Europe. Now go, before you anger me.'

Bruce hesistated for a few seconds, staring uncertainly at the Doctor and desperately anxious to find out what was going on. Finally he lumbered out, followed by the two WZO policemen.

Once they heard the lift doors close out in the lobby, Giles, Victoria and Jamie gathered round the Doctor to congratulate him on his performance.

Giles shook the Doctor's hand vigorously. 'You were fantastic. It worked like a dream,' he cried. 'Are you with us now?'

The Doctor shrugged. 'I don't yet know what you stand for Mr Kent. You and Salamander are clearly on opposite sides, but which side is good and which bad? Why should I interfere?'

'To save the world,' Astrid told him quietly.

'But isn't that exactly what Salamander is trying to do?' Victoria objected.

The Doctor was silently ruffling his hair back into its familiar mop as he wandered across to the wall map. 'Salamander is at present in Central Europe and we are in Australia,' he mused.

Astrid hurried over to join him. 'We can be there in two hours by orbitliner,' she told him, 'and we can start at once.'

Kent bounded over to his desk. 'I have been preparing a plan to infiltrate Salamander's inner circle for some months. It can easily be adapted to suit your two friends,' he said breathlessly, taking some documents from a secret compartment. 'Here are all the necessary travel papers.'

The Doctor looked surprised, and then smiled knowingly. 'Only three intrepid travellers, Mr Kent?' he exclaimed, examining the documents spread over the desk.

Giles nodded. 'Astrid and your two companions.'

Victoria glanced apprehensively at Jamie, but he was

following the proceedings with eager attention.

'Meanwhile, you and I will investigate Salamander's little set-up at Kanowa, Mr Kent,' the Doctor said, adopting his Salamander voice and sending a sudden chill through them all.

Soon after dawn the following morning, Donald Bruce arrived at the Kanowa Research Centre situated in the hills 150 kilometres southwest of Melville. The rising sun glinted majestically on the complex of enormous parabolic dishes and angled mirrors which formed the collector array of Salamander's revolutionary Sunstore system. The installation was scattered over ten square kilometres and was entirely enclosed within a series of buzzing electrified fences. Bruce felt uncomfortable in this mysterious scientific world full of sealed, humming chambers and hazard warning signs. There was something terrifying about the huge solar collectors which turned slowly, tracking the sun as it moved across the sky. Bruce almost shivered as he waited impatiently in the office of the Deputy Director, Theodore Benik.

Eventually Benik arrived. He was shorter than Bruce, with a thin body and a face like the front of a skull. Short black hair straggled across his forehead in a ragged fringe and his large red ears stuck out slightly. Huge eyes burned in deep sockets and the small mouth was drawn tightly over the teeth.

'I'm busy, Bruce. I can spare you ten minutes,' he snapped in his thin high voice. His dislike for the Security Commissioner was completely undisguised.

Bruce controlled himself with difficulty at this blatant disregard for his authority. 'Salamander ... He did go to the Central European Zone?' he asked.

'Well, if *you* don't know, then who does?' Benik replied with heavy sarcasm, glancing through the papers he was carrying. 'Noon orbitliner, day before yesterday,' he added without looking up.

Bruce walked to the window and turned, a large figure silhoutted against the growing daylight. 'I have just flown here from a meeting with Salamander in Melville,' he announced. 'In Giles Kent's office,' Bruce concluded dramatically.

For a moment Benik looked as though he were going to burst out laughing. Then he moved up to the desk and flung down the papers. 'That bastard Kent's got his filthy hands on the Leader,' he shouted, staring wildly at Bruce. 'You incompetent gorilla! Don't you see? He must have some hold over him, right under your nose.'

Bruce remained calm. 'Salamander was in control of the situation. He only needed to bat an eyelid and I'd have knocked off everyone else in sight.'

Benik leaned on the desk, tensed like a dog preparing to spring. 'Something's going on,' he murmured menacingly.

Bruce was glad to have the advantage of the light behind him so that Benik could not detect the uncertainty in his eyes. During the flight to Kanowa he had been forced to admit to himself that Salamander had seemed strangely different during the meeting, and he was worried about the puzzle of the third man seen at Astrid Ferrier's bungalow.

However, he drew himself upright with an authoritative air. 'It is vital to establish that all is well with Salamander,' he told Benik. 'You have direct radio contact with him. Check with him personally when he reaches Budapest for the Conference.'

Benik pointed out that the Leader had ordered that

he was not to be disturbed until the Conference was over.

'All right. As soon as it ends then,' Bruce thundered, 'And let me have a full report as soon as you have spoken to him.'

With that Bruce stamped out of the office.

3

Volcanoes

A heavy gray sky hung over the old Hungarian capital of
Budapest. On the terrace of the ancient Tisza
Palace—now part of the headquarters of the Central
European Zone Authority—three men were deeply
involved in an urgent discussion concerning the threat
of imminent volcanic activity in the area. Two of them,
Alexander Denes, the Zone Controller, and his deputy,
Nicholas Fedorin, were sitting at a wrought-iron table
over which was spread a large geological map of the
Zone. Salamander himself was standing beside them,
indicating various points on the map.

'Volcanic eruptions here?' Denes exclaimed incredulously in a soft Slavonic voice, clasping his pudgy
hands together. He was a plump, fleshy-faced man with
high shoulders and no neck. His eyes were intelligent
and good-humoured. His thinning, wispy gray hair was
combed sideways across the top of his head, which was
large with a high forehead. 'But I cannot believe it, it is
impossible. What do you think, Nicholas?'

His deputy shook his shining bald head emphatically
and tugged at his full, black beard. 'I agree, Alexander.
The whole idea is absurd.' He turned to Salamander.
'Your data must be quite a few degrees out,' he
suggested.

Salamander stiffened. Clenching his fist, he rapped
the map with beringed knuckles. 'I do not think so,

31

Comrade Fedorin,' he snapped. 'So far every single one of my predictions has proved correct.'

Fedorin bowed his head submissively, regretting his rashness. Under the table he clasped his knees with clammy hands.

The Controller smiled blandly and nodded. 'Yes, Salamander, your record has been most impressive, I do not deny,' he murmured pleasantly.

Just then, a small intercom unit placed on the other side of the circular table bleeped several times. Salamander ignored it.

A moment later a tall West Indian girl stepped through the french window onto the terrace. 'Excuse me, Leader, but Communications have just come through to say that ...'

'I gave strict instructions that I was not to be disturbed!' Salamander cried.

The girl turned to go.

'Wait, Fariah. Some refreshments perhaps?' Salamander suggested, turning to the other two men.

Alexander Denes was already levering himself out of his chair. 'Not for me, thank you. I must consult my Scientific Bureau immediately.'

Salamander's mouth formed a smile, but his eyes remained cold. 'Still you do not believe, Alexander.'

The Zone Controller replied that he merely wanted to avoid any false alarms and with a polite bow he turned to leave.

'Your advisers are all amateurs,' Salamander laughed with an exaggerated shrug.

Denes turned back to face him. 'They are extremely skilful and dedicated men, Salamander,' he retorted. 'But they are human and, like all men, they are capable of error.'

Salamander stared after him, obviously needled by Denes' pointed rebuke. Then as Fedorin rose to follow Denes he pushed him firmly back into his seat. 'Stay and drink with me, Comrade, we have much to discuss, you and I,' he purred. 'Fariah, look after the Deputy Controller for a moment.'

Leaving the puzzled man hunched at the table, Salamander hurried into the Palace after Denes, his eyes narrowed in a calculating frown.

Odd spots of rain were beginning to fall as Jamie and Victoria sat waiting on a bench in the Memorial Gardens of the Tisza Park near the Palace. There seemed to be no one about. Large gloomy buildings towered over the trees on the other side of the gray, swiftly flowing river. Victoria was cold and miserable. She felt uneasy without the Doctor. 'Are you sure this is the place?' she mumbled.

Jamie shrugged. 'I'm no sure of anything after that orbital flight jaunt. Third bench. South walk. Memorial Gardens,' he said with a huge yawn. 'Those were the directions, lassie.'

'Well, I don't trust her, Jamie. Suppose it's some kind of a trap?'

Jamie said nothing. He was preoccupied, running over in his mind the details of a daring and dangerous plan in which he would soon be risking his life. Eventually he looked up. Victoria was fast asleep despite the chilly wind. Then he caught sight of a familiar figure strolling casually along the river bank.

It was Astrid. When at last she reached them, she sat down at the other end of the bench without looking at him.

'Denes has arranged everything,' she murmured. 'Salamander is expected to remain at the Palace for only twenty-four hours.' Still staring straight ahead across the river, she put her hand down on the seat and when she took it away there was a small plastic card. 'Your pass. When you enter the Palace, find your way straight to the East Terrace. Then proceed exactly as planned.'

Jamie picked up the pass and palmed it. 'Will you be ready in time, lassie?' he asked anxiously.

Astrid nodded slightly. 'Go now,' she ordered him.

With a glance at Victoria, Jamie got to his feet and sauntered away in the direction Astrid had just come from, whistling a favourite piper's lament.

Victoria woke up with a start, just in time to see him disappearing into the nearby shrubbery. 'Jamie!' she cried, jumping up. 'Where are you going? Come back!'

'Quiet. Sit down,' Astrid hissed savagely. 'Do you want to ruin everything?'

On the East Terrace of the Tisza Palace, barely a kilometre away, Fariah and Fedorin were talking.

'But if you dislike the man, then why do you work for him?' the Deputy asked, sitting down with the drink he had insisted on pouring himself.

A brilliant but ironic smile flashed across the black girl's beautiful face. 'He has a way of persuading people.'

Fedorin nodded innocently. 'Indeed, a most stimulating taskmaster. Salamander seems to radiate a kind of magnetism.' He sipped his drink. 'This is delicious!' he exclaimed.

Fariah smiled again. 'I am very relieved to hear that, Mr Fedorin,' she said pointedly, looking at the glass.

He glanced up at her uncertainly and then stared at his glass in confusion. 'I beg your pardon ...'

'I am Salamander's official food-taster,' she explained, as if the title disgusted her. 'There have been many attempts to poison the Leader.'

'Food-taster!' Fedorin gasped. 'What made you take on such a dangerous job?'

'Hunger!' The word cut through the heavy air like a blade as Salamander came out onto the terrace. 'But it is strange. Now that the girl has all she can eat, she has lost her appetite,' he cried with a brutal laugh. 'Get me a drink, Fariah.'

As she hurried to obey, Fedorin tried to smile. 'You seem to be extremely well protected, sir,' he said.

'Guard!' Salamander yelled. At once a young officer rushed out onto the terrace aiming a lethal-looking gun straight at the terrified Deputy. Fedorin backed slowly away, mesmerised by his own reflection in the guard's glittering vizor.

As the wretched little man collided with the wrought-iron table, Salamander gave a blood-curdling hyena laugh, greatly enjoying the sport. 'Extremely well protected!' he cried. Then his manner changed abruptly and he became charming and polite. 'But have another drink, amigo, and relax,' he purred.

At that moment Jamie appeared, clambering stealthily over the stone parapet at the end of the terrace behind the guard. Fedorin tried to shout a warning, but his voice seemed to be trapped in his throat. He uttered incoherent grunts, gesticulating at the kilted stranger as he jumped from the balustrade. Jamie felled the guard with a single chop to the neck and scooped up the rifle as he landed. Salamander barely had time to turn before finding himself covered at point-blank range. Fariah dropped her tray of drinks with a crash.

'It seems you're not quite as well protected as you like to think,' Jamie told Salamander.

Salamander began reaching carefully for the intercom unit on the table behind him.

'Don't touch that thing if you want to live,' Jamie shouted. He moved cautiously forward, waving them all away from the table and towards the windows. Reaching the table he gingerly picked up the intercom with one hand, keeping his eyes and the gun trained on the retreating huddle of people. 'Now duck!' he cried, kneeling down and hurling the intercom high over the parapet.

As the others flung themselves onto the paving, a stunning explosion rocked the terrace and a huge orange fireball roared into the air. Several windows shattered, showering glass everywhere. The map was sucked off the table and it floated away in pieces. Jamie just caught a glimpse of Astrid through the gaps between the pillars of the parapet as she raced for cover round the corner of the building. 'Well done, ma wee lassie,' he murmured. Then he straightened up and laid the gun on the table.

Three guards ran out of the Palace and advanced on him, their boots crunching over the scattered glass.

'Wait!' Salamander ordered. He walked slowly over to Jamie. 'What is this all about?' he demanded.

Jamie had been preparing himself for his first encounter with the real Salamander for many hours, but even so he found the man's hypnotic gaze hard to resist. 'I ... I heard about a plot, sir,' he mumbled, his mouth feeling dry and sticky. 'A bomb in your intercom. I tried to warn them at the gates, but the Sassenachs wouldn't listen to me.'

Salamander continued to examine him as if he were a specimen in a microscope. 'So how did you get into the Palace?'

Jamie swallowed hard. 'Well, you see, sir, I'm sort of on the road with this friend of mine. She's very pretty, so the sentries didn't spot me slipping by them.'

Salamander walked to the parapet and leaned over. The grass in the paddock below was gouged into a blackened crater. There was no trace of the intercom unit. 'Why did you risk your life for me?' he demanded.

Jamie licked his lips. 'Well, sir, without your leadership I don't think the world has much of a chance,' he answered shyly.

'You are loyal and fearless. That pleases me,' Salamander murmured. 'You would like to work for me?' Salamander adjusted his collar with bejewelled fingers. 'You will not be disappointed by what I pay, I assure you,' he smiled, 'and as for your young lady—no doubt Fariah can find her a task to keep her from mischief.' Salamander clapped his hands with satisfaction. 'You accept?'

Jamie hesitated a moment. 'I'll give it a try, sir,' he grinned. 'But your security arrangements are just terrible. There'll have to be changes.'

Salamander threw back his dark head and laughed throatily. 'Excellent, excellent. We shall discuss everything later. Fariah, take our new young warrior and feed him. Find him a uniform and then bring him and his young lady to me.'

Furious with Jamie for not telling her what was happening, Victoria had been sitting alone for what seemed like hours on the bench in the Memorial

37

Gardens. As the sky became more and more overcast, she grew more and more afraid.

At last Astrid returned and sat silently at the other end of the beach pretending to read a newspaper. Victoria soon reached the point of wanting to snatch it out of her hands and hurl it into the river. She did not understand why they could not at least speak to each other.

Suddenly Jamie appeared, whistling jauntily as he strode through the shrubbery. He sat down between the two girls. 'It worked. They think I saved Salamander's life,' he murmured.

'You might have been followed,' Astrid warned, without looking up.

Jamie revealed that Salamander had offered him a job.

'Perfect, Jamie. You're a genius,' Astrid said.

Suddenly she stuffed the newspaper into her shoulder bag and got up. 'Danger!' she whispered, before setting off along the river bank towards a distant marina situated downstream of them.

'That lassie has eyes in the back of her head,' Jamie muttered, catching sight of two people emerging from the shrubbery. As they neared the bench, he suddenly spoke in a loud, casual voice as if he were in the midst of a conversation. '... and so he says there's a job for both of us ...'

They were confronted by Fariah and a Palace security officer.

'Who was that woman you were talking to just now?' the officer demanded.

'We weren't. She was just sitting there,' Victoria retorted bitterly.

'The boy had no right to leave the Palace,' the officer

shouted. 'And who is this vagrant?' he inquired, staring at Victoria.

Fariah cast her eyes skywards. 'I have already explained, Captain,' she said patiently. 'Mr McCrimmon came to collect his friend. Salamander ordered it.'

The Captain stared suspiciously after Astrid's receding figure. Then he glared at Victoria and finally at Jamie. 'I shall check with the Leader personally,' he rapped.

Fariah ignored him and introduced herself to Victoria. 'You just come along with me,' she smiled reassuringly.

As they walked through the deserted, gloomy park towards the Tisza Palace, the Captain followed a short distance behind them. He was speaking rapidly and quietly into his walkie-talkie, occasionally glancing round at the forest of masts waving forlornly in the distance.

Concealed in the maze of wooden struts beneath the outer end of the marina jetty, Astrid waited. She tried to keep calm. The operation on the East Terrace had been blessed with incredible luck: she had only just managed to reach cover behind a small buttress before the explosive she had planted had detonated; then she had run the gauntlet of the Palace security guards. She was still shaking, and wondering how much longer the luck was going to last.

She took a small automatic out of her bag and checked its magazine as she heard stealthy movements coming from the landward end of the jetty. Eventually Alexander Denes appeared, clambering laboriously through the tangle of beams towards her. Panting heavily, he squeezed his generous bulk into the angled stanchions beside her. 'Have we been successful?' he whispered anxiously.

'Salamander's swallowed it so far. The boy is very capable, but the girl could be a liability.'

Denes stared down at the rushing water and sighed. 'I had not met Salamander before,' he frowned. 'You and Giles are right about him, Astrid. He must be stopped. But I hate the idea of violence.'

Astrid put her hand on his arm. 'He'll be stopped—somehow. I must get back to Giles tonight. Things should be starting to happen at the Australian end by now. Can you hold on here until the boy gets the information we need?'

Denes nodded. 'With a little luck. I think I can trust Nicholas, weak as he is.'

Astrid clambered up to check that the coast was clear, then slid back into her niche. 'You'd better go, Alex,' she said gently. 'I'll wait ten minutes before I leave. Keep your eye on Fedorin.'

The Zone Controller smiled. 'You take care as well, my dear.' He leaned forward and kissed her on the cheek and she pressed his hand reassuringly. Then he heaved himself round and began to manoeuvre his way clumsily back towards the river bank.

As darkness fell, Salamander and Fedorin had been sitting alone in the lofty, ornate salon leading off the East Terrace. The hapless Deputy Controller had been steadily drinking and protesting his innocence, while Salamander revealed that he possessed cast-iron proof that Fedorin had been involved in elaborate interzonal fraud.

40

Now he followed Salamander out onto the chilly terrace clutching yet another full glass, his head thick and spinning. 'But this ... this is a conspiracy a ... against me ...' he stammered, gasping in the sudden fresh air. 'Some anarchist plot ... to ruin me.'

'My dear Nicholas, what do you take me for?' Salamander murmured soothingly. 'I do not intend to expose your crimes in public. It is an insurance.' He turned to face his swaying victim, his eyes and his teeth gleaming in the twilight. 'You just have to do something for me ...' he smiled.

Fedorin took a large swig from his glass. 'What?'

'Just a little thing. You are going to take the place of Alexander Denes. You will become Central European Controller.'

Fedorin grabbed the edge of the table for support and pushed his sliding spectacles back up his sweating nose. He gulped some more brandy. 'But Alexander ... Alexander,' he faltered groggily.

Salamander leaned over the table, his unblinking eyes burning. 'Ah yes, the well-respected Denes,' he murmured, 'the humane bureaucrat. Such a pity. The man is going to die, Fedorin. Mysteriously.'

Fedorin drained his glass with a shudder. 'You can't make me do that,' he whispered, the brandy overflowing down his chin and staining his tunic.

Salamander glanced at his watch. 'Oh, I think I can *ask* you to do anything I wish, amigo. And my predictions are always accurate.'

At that moment the terrace suddenly shook violently. The tall windows and the glasses on the table rattled loudly, and a deep rumbling sound echoed across the city.

Salamander turned and peered through the image-intensifying binoculars he was carrying slung round his neck. 'The Eperjest Tokyar Range is about to erupt. It should be quite spectacular,' he announced.

Fedorin glanced from the back of Salamander's head to the heavy chair beside him. For a moment his befuddled brain struggled to command his unsteady body to act while it had the chance.

But the opportunity slipped away for ever as Salamander swung round on him. 'This will be a disaster for the Zone,' he declared triumphantly. 'I cannot prevent it, but I shall come to the aid of the people in their misfortune.'

'And take over. The Zone will be yours.'

'Ours, my dear Nicholas, ours,' Salamander corrected him. 'I offer you partnership. You will have half or you will have nothing at all. Choose.'

Again the terrace shuddered and creaked as more tremors rippled across the city. Salamander scanned the horizon eagerly. The sky above the mountains had begun to glow a dull faint orange and occasional flashes burst like lightning along the skyline.

'Come and look,' he cried, 'it is most beautiful. The glorious power of nature to change the world ...'

Before Fedorin could move there was a commotion inside the salon and Donald Bruce strode out onto the terrace with two of his WZO policemen.

Salamander stared at him in surprised irritation. 'What are you doing here, Bruce?' he demanded.

The Security Chief was clearly out of breath. 'I came as soon as I could,' he panted. 'The attempt on your life ... there will be arrests within the hour, I can assure you.'

Salamander nodded impatiently. 'My dear Bruce, my own personal guards are already dealing with the

42

incident. At present I am occupied with more serious matters.' He offered the special binoculars to Bruce and pointed to the glowing horizon. 'A terrible disaster, I fear. The Eperjest Tokyar Region. We shall need to mount a comprehensive relief operation at dawn.'

Bruce squinted through the glasses at the ruddy glow in the distance. 'You certainly have the knack of being in the right place at the right time, sir,' he murmured.

There was another flurry of activity inside and Alexander Denes stormed onto the terrace. Under the ornate lanterns his face looked like chalk and his usually kind eyes were blazing with anger. 'What have you done? What have you done?' he cried, going straight up to Salamander as if to attack him physically.

Salamander looked completely taken aback. He turned to Donald Bruce with eyebrows raised and then back to Denes. 'But I warned you, Alexander. I warned you on this very spot this afternoon,' he protested, 'eruptions in Eperjest Tokyar ...'

'But how could you *know*?' Denes shouted. He looked round at Donald Bruce, at Fedorin and at the two policemen. 'Somehow this monster has engineered this catastrophe in Eperjest Tokyar,' he told them, his hands clenching and unclenching helplessly. 'There has been no volcanic activity there for hundreds of thousands of years and no seismological warning whatsoever.'

A third time the terrace vibrated violently. A strange burning smell was beginning to drift over the Palace and everyone turned to watch the eerie glow over the mountains intensifying steadily.

Denes was breathing heavily with a painful wheezing and choking sound. 'I do not know how you have done this terrible crime to innocent people,' he whispered hoarsely, 'but I am convinced that it is for your own ends and I shall demand ...'

Salamander cut short Denes' outburst. Wrenching himself free, he turned to Donald Bruce. 'Arrest this man!' he ordered.

There was a stunned silence, broken only by the distant thunder of the volcanic eruptions and the rattling of the salon windows.

Donald Bruce shook his head and stared sullenly at his feet. 'What is the charge, sir?' he asked reluctantly.

The whites of Salamander's eyes flashed menacingly. 'Criminal incompetence, slander and treason,' he snapped.

Alexander Denes gazes around him as if he were dreaming. 'This is an outrage. The charges are absurd.' He started laughing as if the whole thing were a practical joke. 'Fedorin, what is all this nonsense?' he cried.

His Deputy looked at the ground and said nothing.

Salamander spoke in a quietly chilling voice, 'My dear Denes, at your trial Senor Fedorin will be the chief witness for the prosecution.'

4

Too Many Cooks

Ordering Fedorin to accompany him, Salamander entered the Palace saying that he had urgent emergency relief plans to prepare and reports to submit to WZO Headquarters in Geneva. Donald Bruce was left with the prisoner and escort on the terrace, which continued to shake at regular intervals as the earth tremors spread with each eruption.

'If you please, Mr Denes ...' Bruce mumbled unhappily, indicating that he should move into the Palace.

As he followed them in, Bruce caught sight of a hefty figure wearing the uniform of a Lieutenant in Salamander's own Security Corps. 'McCrimmon! What are you doing dressed like this?' he exclaimed in astonishment.

'Leader's orders,' Jamie replied sharply.

Bruce ignored the implied insult. 'I want to know what Salamander and Giles Kent were discussing in Melville yesterday,' he said.

'Confidential,' Jamie snapped, turning to leave.

Bruce controlled himself with great difficulty. 'I am responsible for law and order. Kent is suspected of being a serious danger to Salamander.'

Jamie shrugged. 'If the Leader wants you to know why he was with Kent, he'll tell you himself,' he retorted. 'But I canna stand here gossiping. This Zone has been declared a disaster area, you know. There's a lot to do.'

With this piece of devastating impudence Jamie marched out of the salon, leaving the Security Commissioner gaping in silent and impotent rage.

Salamander and Fedorin were standing by a small wall-safe in a dark, heavily furnished room which formed part of Salamander's accommodation during his visit to the Zone.

'It's blackmail!' Fedorin protested, as Salamander carefully replaced two bulging files in the cavity behind an ornate clock which stood on the huge mantelpiece.

'Nonsense. I am actually suppressing these damaging facts about your past,' Salamander retorted. 'I am making you into Central European Supremo!'

Fedorin took off his horn rimmed glasses and tried to clean them on his sleeve, blinking at Salamander in the gloom. 'I could never give evidence against Alexander in court. His lawyers would tie me in knots.'

Salamander laughed. 'Lawyers? Court? All non-sense, my dear Nicholas,' he purred soothingly, taking a small plastic box from the safe and pressing it into Fedorin's clammy, trembling hand. 'This is so much less troublesome. Use it wisely and your future is made. Such a small risk. And the insurance is more than adequate,' Salamander said, sliding the heavy clock back against the chimney breast. He moved the hands back and forth around the clockface in a complicated sequence until there was a whirring sound followed by a sharp click. The clock chimed prettily and then struck the hour.

Salamander snapped the glass cover shut. 'And

remember, amigo—there is no time like the present.'

In the medieval kitchens situated in the basement of the Palace, Victoria and Fariah were talking to a leathery-faced, shrivelled little man dressed in a rather overelaborate chef's outfit as he prepared dinner for his master and guests. This was Griffin, Salamander's personal chef.

'I've got just the job for you,' Griffin croaked, with a sour grin at Victoria. 'Peel them spuds.' He stuffed his hat into his apron. 'I'm going for a walk—to look for inspiration. It'll probably rain,' he mumbled, shuffling out of the kitchen.

Victoria rolled up her sleeves and set to work on the mound of potatoes in the sink. 'Griffin doesn't like me, I'm afraid,' she said.

Suddenly her arm was taken in a fierce grip. Dropping the knife, she found herself looking into Fariah's gleaming eyes.

'You must get away from here,' the black girl murmured earnestly. 'Don't let yourself be corrupted by Salamander's evil world.'

Unnoticed by the two girls, Jamie had slipped stealthily into the kitchen and was standing listening in the shadows.

Victoria stared at Fariah in astonishment. 'Whatever do you mean?' she exclaimed. 'You don't sound very loyal to your Leader.'

'Loyal?' Fariah almost spat. 'Loyal?' Her lithe body tensed as she sensed the presence of someone else. 'Finish these vegetables by the time I return,' Fariah ordered and abruptly strode out.

Seeing the young Corps Lieutenant watching her, Victoria seized the knife and resumed her task with exaggerated eagerness. A moment later her arm was again gripped, this time by a black-gloved hand. She recognised Jamie's smiling face with great relief.

'I managed to slip out and tell Astrid what's happened before she left for Australia,' Jamie told her. He explained that Astrid was going to try to rescue Alexander Denes and take him to Australia with her. 'She thinks the Doctor will believe Denes more than anyone else,' he said.

Victoria looked doubtful. 'Rescue Denes? But Salamander's guards are everywhere.'

Jamie grinned. 'You don't have to tell *me*!'

'Giles Kent was right. Salamander is an evil man. You can just sense it everywhere,' Victoria murmured.

As briefly as he could, Jamie told her what he had overheard on the terrace concerning the conspiracy against Denes.

Victoria listened incredulously. 'Do you really mean that Salamander actually caused the disaster so that he could take over the Zone?' she exclaimed, when he had finished. 'But Jamie, how on earth could he do that?'

Kent's large motor caravan was parked on the edge of a thicket near the perimeter fence of the Kanowa Research Centre. Inside, Kent and the Doctor gazed in horror at the screen of a small portable television which was showing an interzonal newsflash of the catastrophe in the Hungarian mountains. When the bulletin ended, Kent switched off and they sat there in appalled silence.

Eventually Kent reached for a can of beer and ripped the top open savagely. 'I'm sure Salamander's responsible for those eruptions,' he muttered.

The Doctor shook his head. 'I am not convinced,

Kent.' He got up and walked about in the neat but confined space, deep in thought. 'You are asking me to believe that Salamander has found a way to harness and control vast geophysical forces. It's not impossible of course, but I need to know more.' He picked up a pair of powerful binoculars from the small table and parted the curtains drawn tightly over one of the windows. He studied the Research Centre closely, scanning the enormous solar collectors and mirrors, and began to make a series of complex mental calculations while muttering quietly to himself. 'What was it that aroused your suspicions?' he asked at last.

'It was the requisition papers for supplies to the Centre that I managed to get hold of. They didn't make sense, Doctor. Salamander was ordering enough materials and provisions for a small town. He was obviously getting finance from the World Zones Monetary Fund for some other big scheme besides the Sunstore.'

The Doctor shut the curtains and sat down. 'Evidence!' he exclaimed, his eyes lighting up. 'You have the documents? Photocopies?' he asked eagerly.

'All destroyed, Doctor. I was accused of malicious conspiracy and disgraced.'

'Something of a Jekyll and Hyde character, our friend Salamander,' the Doctor mused. 'I'm most impatient to hear what Jamie and Victoria have discovered.'

Suddenly Kent leapt to the window set into the door of the caravan. The Doctor heard the turbojet of a hovercar approaching rapidly.

'Damn Benik!' Kent breathed, closing the curtain and rushing across to one of the divans. He lifted it like a lid, revealing a coffin-like space underneath. 'Quick. In here, Doctor,' he snapped.

After a moment's hesitation, the Doctor clambered in and wriggled himself into a lying position. 'I do hate this cloak and dagger business,' he muttered as Kent slammed the bed down.

The sound of the hovercar reached a climax and then moaned into silence as the vehicle came to rest outside. Then there was a splintering crash as the door was almost yanked off its hinges. A burly guard from Salamander's Security Corps burst in, followed by the Deputy Director of the Kanowa Research Centre.

'I might have known,' Benik said acidly.

'I'm honoured,' Giles replied mildly. 'I didn't expect a visit from the Deputy Director himself. You have a warrant for this intrusion of course.'

'Not necessary, Kent. You are on Research Centre territory,' Benik retorted in a deliberately clipped voice.

Giles held up an ordnance map. 'Just outside the boundary. Check if you like.'

A stickler for regulations when it suited him, Benik simmered quietly. 'What are you doing here?' he demanded, snatching up the binoculars and wrenching open the curtains at one of the windows. 'Bird-watching?'

Kent nodded. 'It's the best time to see needle-tailed swift, Pacific golden plover and Arctic tern,' he said coolly. 'If you're interested in such things.'

Benik turned. 'I am interested in whatever you are interested in, Kent. An excellent view of the Centre from here.'

'Not bad,' Giles agreed.

Benik attempted a broad smile, with hideous results. 'You won't be staying in the area, will you?'

'I'll stay as long as I like, Benik.'

At a glance from Benik, the security guard started to smash up the interior of the caravan with the butt of his high-velocity rifle. Crockery, kitchen utensils, jars and packets of food were sent flying in all directions. When Kent tried to intervene he was tossed aside.

The assault was brief but devastating. As the guard marched to the door and stood at attention, Benik gloated over his handiwork with a crazed smile. 'No sense in complaining to the authorities,' he hissed. 'No one will believe you, will they?'

Benik and the guard went out. Doors slammed and the hovercar screamed away into the distance, its siren droning.

Kent opened up the divan and helped the Doctor out of his hiding place. After surveying the shambles in dismay, the Doctor picked up some fragments of crockery and tried to fit them together. 'Isn't it a pity, Kent,' he murmured sadly. 'People spend their time creating beautiful things and other people come along and simply destroy them.'

Giles grasped the Doctor firmly by the arm. 'Look around you,' he cried fervently. 'Surely you understand now. Surely you can see what kind of man Salamander is.'

The Doctor held up the broken pieces of china. 'This is exactly what we need, Kent. More evidence. More facts. And that is precisely what I hope Jamie and Victoria are going to bring us.'

In the basement kitchen Jamie was eating heartily at the huge scrubbed table, while Victoria busied herself laying a small trolley with cutlery and plates. Suddenly Astrid slipped in.

51

'You got through!' Jamie cried admiringly with his mouth full. 'Och, that's ma we lassie! What's next?'

Astrid explained in a low, urgent voice, 'Salamander is impatient, but he won't act until he has dealt with Denes once and for all. At the moment he's tied up with the emergency in the mountains so we must get Alexander out of here as soon as possible.'

'There are guards everywhere,' Jamie pointed out.

'Exactly. All you have to do is to cause a distraction Jamie, anything you like, but it must happen at precisely 23.00 hours. I shall try to get Alexander out of the Palace and take him with me to Australia on the night flight. It's vital he meets your friend the Doctor now.'

Jamie nodded. 'I'll raise hell at eleven,' he promised, taking a mighty bite out of the sandwich Victoria had made for him.

At that moment Griffin came shuffling in with two bottles of claret in each hand.

'Down the passage and third on the right. Thank you,' Astrid said loudly to Jamie, sweeping past the little chef and out of the kitchen.

As Victoria backed out of the antiquated lift with the trolley bearing Denes' supper, a man with a full black beard and heavy horn-rimmed glasses suddenly appeared behind her. In the dim light from the small chandeliers strung along the corridor the figure was momentarily terrifying.

The little man bowed, his uneasily shifty eyes enlarged grotesquely by the thick lenses. His forehead was beaded with sweat. 'I am Nicholas Fedorin,' he replied formally. 'I am ... I was Alexander Denes'

52

Deputy. Is this for Mr Denes?'

'I'm just taking it to him,' Victoria said, now more wary than frightened.

Fedorin lifted one of the heavy silver dishcovers. 'Delicious,' he murmured. He scanned the trolley. 'Fresh bread!' he exclaimed. Victoria glanced at the generous slices and as she did so, Fedorin's hand closed unnoticed round the saltcellar. 'Ah, you must be new here, you have forgotten the salt!' he cried.

Victoria stared at the trolley with a puzzled frown. 'Oh, but I'm quite sure I ...'

'Please run down and bring the salt. Mr Denes is most particular,' Fedorin interrupted her, pressing the lift button.

As soon as the doors had closed behind Victoria, he slipped the saltcellar into his pocket and after glancing furtively up and down the seemingly endless corridor he took out the small box which Salamander had given him earlier.

With violently trembling fingers, he opened it and stared at the pale green crystals for a moment. Then he lifted the lid of the soup tureen and held the box over the steaming liquid. Immediately his spectacles misted over. Dropping the lid with an echoing clatter, he whipped them off and peered at the poison crystals, shaking the box slightly. The crystals seemed to have got stuck together in a mass. With a whimper of frustration, Fedorin shook the box and the congealed green substance fell out onto the tray, splitting into several smaller lumps.

Just then a door slammed loudly nearby. Uttering strangled little cries of terror like a trapped child, Fedorin hastily tried to pick up the solidified lumps and put them back in the box, while peering blindly around

In the salon Salamander walked slowly round and round his victim, speaking in a voice hushed with menace and contempt.

'I give you the chance to become somebody at last and you let it slip out of your boneless fingers. I create this golden chance for you, and you come whimpering back to me like an infant,' he murmured. 'I think you do not understand what is at stake, amigo.'

Fedorin mopped his face and replaced his spectacles. 'There must be another way,' he gasped, shielding his eyes from the intense glare of the lamps. 'These crystals, I could not do it. I stood there with Alexander's life in my hands and I could not do it.'

Salamander took the small box from Fedorin's clammy hand and went over to a side table in the shadows. 'Of course I understand, amigo,' he said in a suddenly soothing tone. 'Try not to reproach yourself. We try, we fail. So, the moon does not fall out of the sky.' Keeping his back turned, Salamander poured two drinks.

The helpless Deputy screwed up his eyes, trying to follow Salamander's movements round the dim edges of his vision. 'We ... we will find another way?' he faltered.

'Later, later,' Salamander cried, bringing over two glasses. 'Cheer up and have a drink, Nicholas. We can discuss some other strategy tomorrow.'

Fedorin eagerly accepted the proffered glass.

'Your health,' Salamander said encouragingly, drinking from his glass.

Fedorin took a sip and gave a sickly smile. He took

another sip. Suddenly he stared at Salamander in horror. His glass fell to the floor and he lurched forward, grabbing at the back of a chair for support. His spectacles slipped off his nose and his knees buckled.

With a spine-chilling gurgling sound, he shuddered and slid to his knees with his arms over the back of the chair. For a few seconds Salamander looked at the broken figure kneeling there with splayed arms and open-mouthed stare like a discarded puppet. 'I warned you, amigo,' he breathed, 'only one chance.' Then he picked up the almost empty box of crystals from the drinks table, snapped the lid shut and stuffed it into the dead man's pocket. He nudged Fedorin's shoulder and the corpse toppled sideways, dragging the chair on top of itself.

There was a sharp knock at the door and the Captain entered. 'Excuse me, Leader. An incident in the grounds. Lieutenant McCrimmon reports seeing an intruder near ...' He broke off as he noticed Fedorin's crooked body at Salamander's feet.

'Get Bruce!' Salamander snapped, moving swiftly towards the door. 'And get that cleared up!' he added. 'Very sad. Such a waste.' And he was gone.

5

Seeds of Suspicion

Jamie was hunched in the alcove of an open window in the basement kitchen, aiming his high-velocity rifle through the bars at something in the darkness outside. Griffin was peering over his shoulder looking sceptical.

'You've bin drinkin', my lad. There's nobody out there,' he muttered.

'Look. Over there by the trees,' Jamie insisted. 'He's armed too. Get away from the window, Griff. I'm going out there.' Jamie ran to the small door leading out into the paddock, slid back the rusting bolts and eased his way through.

There was a sharp crack outside as Jamie fired deliberately into the air. Griffin scampered across to the window.

There was a second crack as Jamie fired into the air again. Griffin ducked beneath the sill. 'Why did I ever leave the Old Kent Road?' he grumbled, covering his ears.

A third shot was followed by a whining ricochet and fragments of window-frame flew across the kitchen. Immediately afterwards a dozen armed guards from the Security Corps crashed into the kitchen from the inside door and raced out through the door leading into the grounds.

Out in the paddock Jamie was lurking near the trees, keeping a watchful eye on the Palace and anxiously wondering whether his desperate ruse could possibly succeed. Suddenly a group of guards appeared through the door below the terrace and a powerful searchlight cut through the darkness from somewhere up on the roof of the Palace. It raked the area around the trees until it picked him out.

Yelling to the approaching guards to keep down, Jamie flung himself into the damp grass and trained his rifle on the trees. But the searchlight beam stayed on him. In a few moments he found himself looking up the barrels of a dozen assorted guns.

Getting slowly to his feet Jamie nodded towards the trees. 'I think he got away,' he muttered lamely.

In the gloomy lobby where Alexander Denes was awaiting transfer to prison, Victoria was growing more and more apprehensive as she glanced out of the corner of her eye at the seconds blinking away on the prisoner's wristwatch. She was desperate to warn him about the rescue attempt planned for 23.00 hours, but she could not think of a way to distract the two WZO police officers who stood watching Denes quietly eating his supper with dignified calm.

All at once several armed guards came sprinting through the lobby. Victoria took advantage of the brief distraction to whisper rapidly to Denes, 'Astrid's trying to get you away from here,' but before she could say more, Astrid appeared suddenly round a corner and ran lightly up to them.

'Quick. An attempt is being made to rescue this man,' she rapped at the two startled policemen. 'The Leader instructs us to transfer him at once!'

As the officers glanced at each other in confusion,

Astrid hit one of them expertly on the back of the neck and pushed his collapsing body hard against the other one. Then she grabbed Denes by the arm and started to propel him along the corridor leading to the main entrance of the Palace. Scarcely aware of what she was doing, Victoria seized the heavy soup tureen from the tray and flung it with all her might at the sprawling policemen, knocking the second one out cold.

Just then the Security Corps Captain came racing down the long corridor towards the lobby. 'Stop, Denes! Stop!' he shouted, raising his machine pistol as he ran. Before Astrid could drag Denes round the corner into the entrance hall, he was hit in the back by a short burst from the Captain's gun. He threw up his arms with a gasp, but he managed to stagger out of sight as Astrid caught him round the waist and half carried him along, moaning with agony.

Other guards appeared in the corridor behind the Captain and joined the pursuit. As they reached the lobby, Victoria gave the trolley an almighty shove and sent it careering straight into the leading pursuers. Those following behind tripped over their tumbling colleagues in a tangle of rifles, plates, pistols and cutlery.

For a moment Victoria stood rooted to the spot, almost hypnotised by the devastating effect of her action and deafened by the noise.

Scrambling to his feet, the Captain kicked at the heap of struggling guards surrounding him. 'Get after them, you incompetent buffoons,' he screamed from behind his fogged-up vizor. As they obeyed, Victoria found herself starting to giggle hysterically at the pantomime. But her hysteria died at once as the Captain strode towards her, his pistol pointing between her eyes.

'You are under arrest, Miss Waterfield,' he hissed, grabbing her brutally by the arm. 'You have a lot of questions to answer.'

As the two fugitives struggled along the short corridor into the entrance hall, Denes staggered and fell against the wall. 'I can't ... you run ... leave me ...' he gasped, blood frothing from his mouth and a bright red stain spreading rapidly over the back of his tunic.

Astrid fought to help him to his feet. 'Try, Alexander, you must try,' she cried desperately. But Denes was too heavy for her and too weak to move himself.

'Run, my dear, run,' Denes panted, the faintest shadow of a smile flickering on his deathly pale cheeks. 'It is finished for me now. You must win, you and Giles must ...' Denes was gripped in a final agonised convulsion and then lay still.

Astrid hesitated for a second longer, blinking back tears of frustration and sadness. An instant later the guards hurtled round the corner and Astrid spun round and ran for her life through the elegant hallway of the Tisza Palace.

When Victoria was marched into the salon by the Captain, she found Jamie already facing Salamander and Donald Bruce across the vast banqueting table, which had been cleared except for a solitary rifle lying in the centre.

'Ah. Our little party is almost complete!' Salamander observed as Victoria was thrust next to Jamie. 'We lack only your attractive lady accomplice.'

'I dinna ken what you mean,' exclaimed Jamie, doing

his best to sound genuinely indignant.

'Your accomplice in the abortive plot to free Denes,' Salamander rapped in a staccato voice. 'She has temporarily eluded us. But not for long.'

'What's all this about a plot?' Jamie demanded.

Donald Bruce spoke in a quiet monotone, his flashing spectacles the only visible part of his features. 'Your lunatic scheme to cause a diversion. We know there was no intruder in the grounds, McCrimmon.'

'A saw somebody out there. Three shots were fired at me,' he shouted.

Bruce nodded grimly and picked up the rifle from the table between them. 'Yes, three shots have indeed been fired,' he murmured. 'From this weapon. *Your* gun, McCrimmon.'

Suddenly Salamander swung round on Donald Bruce. 'I come here to this European Zone,' he cried, 'and a bogus attempt on my life is staged. The Zone Controller is exposed as criminally incompetent and his Deputy commits suicide because I confront him with his past crimes. I come into a madhouse infested with conspiracies—and all this time innocent people are suffering in their thousands in a terrible holocaust a few kilometres away. It is a farce. A nightmare. Bruce, you are responsible for world security. Just for once in your life, do your job!'

Donald Bruce stared at Jamie and Victoria as if he could scarcely wait to take revenge on them for being the cause of this humiliating outburst against him. He barked an order and they were marched roughly out of the salon, surrounded by the heavily armed guards.

'None of this makes any sense at all,' he complained wearily, as soon as he and Salamander were alone. 'Yesterday I see you with McCrimmon, the Waterfield girl, Astrid Ferrier and Giles Kent in Kent's office in Melville, all engaged on some secret business or other. And now today I find you ...'

Bruce broke off abruptly. Salamander had seized his arm in an iron grip and was staring at him with fanatical intensity.

'What are you saying, Bruce?' he demanded hoarsely. 'I have not seen Giles Kent for months. And yesterday I was here.'

'But you were with him yesterday in his office. I spoke to you there,' Bruce insisted. 'In fact I thought it so extraordinary that I went to Kanowa and talked to Benik about it. Then I came straight here to Budapest to check that you ...'

Bruce fell silent. Salamander was no longer listening.

'But if it wasn't you, Leader ...' Bruce began.

'Who was it?' Salamander whispered icily.

For the very first time since he had known Salamander Bruce suddenly saw him shaken and on the defensive. He knew that just as a cornered animal can become instantly ferocious, a man like Salamander could become a terrible threat once he was trapped. No one would be safe.

For several seconds neither of them moved. Then Salamander released Bruce's arm and stabbed the button of the intercom on the table beside him. 'I am returning to Kanowa immediately!' he announced. 'And you will accompany me, Bruce. Together we shall track down this imposter and unmask him ...'

In the caravan Giles Kent went over and checked the aerial connection on the small videophone which he had taken from a concealed cupboard after Benik's

61

departure and set up ready for receiving Astrid's progress reports from Europe.

'Something's gone wrong. We should've heard from her by now,' he muttered fatalistically. 'If only we could call her up somehow.'

The Doctor took the binoculars and scanned the Research Centre again. 'I fear we shall have to sit it out here, Kent. But I doubt that our friend Mr Benik will allow us to perch here for much longer unmolested.'

At that moment the videophone warbled quietly. For a moment the Doctor and Giles simply looked at one another, then Giles lunged across the caravan and snapped a series of switches.

On the small screen a haze of static jerkily resolved into Astrid's face. As the picture sharpened they were shocked to see that she looked tired and haggard, her face was streaked with sweat and her normally well-groomed hair was all over the place.

Before the Doctor could stop him, Giles greeted her with delighted relief. 'Astrid, we'd almost given you up. Where are you?'

The Doctor shoved him aside and spoke into the screen with quiet urgency. 'Astrid, switch to *scramble* immediately. Do you hear me? *Scramble.*'

Astrid stared for a second and then suddenly pulled herself together. 'Of course. Switching now,' she murmured. Her face was replaced by a zigzag jumble of lines and the speaker emitted a meaningless buzzing.

'I'm sorry. Sheer carelessness,' Giles mumbled as he watched the Doctor tuning the decoder unit on the side of the videophone, 'but I was getting so worried.'

The Doctor nodded sympathetically, but there was an uneasy frown on his face as he brought Astrid back onto the screen. 'From now on none of us can be too careful, Mr Kent,' he said without looking round.

Having engaged the scrambler circuit, Astrid sat wearily in Giles Kent's swivel chair and, still trying to recover her breath, recounted the events of the last twenty-four hours into the videophone on the desk. She watched the Doctor's face growing graver and graver and Giles Kent finally putting his head in his hands as she described Alexander Denes' arrest and murder.

'Alexander dead,' Kent muttered, 'Jeez, that's tragic.'

'Shot in the back,' Astrid nodded, her voice slow and heavy with fatigue. 'I'm so sorry, Giles, I'm afraid I haven't done very well, have I?'

The Doctor tried to give a reassuring smile. 'You are not to blame, my dear, you did your best,' he said. His gentle face was deeply lined with anxiety. 'So you have no news of Victoria and Jamie?' he inquired after a long silence.

Astrid shook her head. There was another silence.

Suddenly Giles roused himself and with an effort snapped out of his depression. 'Listen, Astrid, at least you're safe. Stay where you are and we'll meet you there in Melville as quickly as we can.'

Before Astrid could answer, the screen went blank. She switched off and lay back in the adjustable chair, no longer fighting the drowsiness which had been creeping over her since she had disembarked from the interzonal orbiter. She rapidly sank into a deep sleep.

After a while there was a noise out in the lobby as the lift doors opened and then shut again. Part of Astrid's mind had remained alert and she jerked awake in time to see the handle of the outer office door starting to turn.

She was on her feet in a flash and she ran lightly across the office and positioned herself behind the slowly opening door. With a sudden wrench, she flung it wide and hurled someone bodily into the room. She threw herself onto the intruder and they crashed violently against the heavy desk.

To her astonishment Astrid found herself staring into the large startled eyes of Fariah, as she pinned her firmly down onto the desk top.

'What are *you* doing here?' she cried.

The black girl clawed frantically at Astrid's hands which were clamped round her throat like a vice. 'I can't talk if you choke ... me,' she gasped.

Astrid manoeuvred her victim round the desk so that she could grab her small automatic from the bag slung over the chair. Then, covering Fariah with the gun, she backed across the office and flicked the door shut with her foot.

Fariah gazed back at Astrid with calm defiance. 'You think Salamander sent me' she said after a tense pause. 'I came to see Giles Kent. I have information for him. Something really big.'

Astrid laughed cynically, walking slowly forward until just the desk was between them. 'It's ridiculous. Why should you help Giles?'

'Because I hate Salamander!' Fariah spat the name out as if it were poisonous. 'Because I hate Salamander more deeply than any of you. Because I have something which will help to destroy him. And I want to be there,' she murmured fervently, 'I want to be there to see the monster's face when he realises he is finished for ever ...'

Theodore Benik's mean eyes had lit up with anticipation

64

when the interceptor module connected to his video-phone flashed up Astrid's transmission to Giles Kent on the screen in his office at the Kanowa Research Centre. 'Now perhaps we shall discover what our bird-watcher is really up to,' he muttered. But his delight turned to rage when the screen suddenly went haywire and the speaker emitted a babble of nonsense.

'Scrambled!' he snarled, stabbing viciously at the switches in a fruitless attempt to restore the picture or at least to get back the sound signal. Eventually he gave up and called the Security Department. It took a few seconds for the image of the duty officer to flicker onto the screen.

'Is everyone asleep over there?' Benik snapped. 'Listen, the girl Astrid Ferrier is somewhere in this Zone. There is an identiprint in Records. I want her traced. Top priority. Inform me the moment she is located.'

The guard nodded and the screen went blank. While Benik waited, he tried to occupy himself with all the reports which Salamander would insist on examining the instant he returned to Kanowa. The Deputy Director was desperately anxious to get to the bottom of Giles Kent's activities and to prevent any trouble occuring while he was temporarily in charge of the Centre. His impatience grew with every minute that passed without news from Security. When at last the officer flashed back onto the screen, Benik was wound up like a tight spring.

'What the hell have you all been doing?' he screamed.

The officer remained impassive as he informed him that Astrid Ferrier had travelled to the Central European Zone and then returned that morning.

'Central Europe,' Benik murmured, his eyes narrowing. For a moment he was silent. 'Where is she now?' he demanded abruptly.

'A woman of her description was seen by one of our agents entering Giles Kent's office in Melville, sir,' the guard replied.

'Was she alone?'

'Yes, sir. But shortly afterwards someone else followed her into the building.'

'Who?' Benik screamed, almost beside himself. 'Who was it?'

'The Leader's personal food-taster, sir.'

'Fariah,' Benik murmured, lingering over the name menacingly. 'I want that place surrounded at once. No one must be permitted to leave do you understand? And I want a turbocar in two minutes.'

The guard looked confused. 'Shall I contact the WZO police, sir?'

'Just do as I order. Take your best men,' Benik snapped.

The officer nodded. 'And excuse me, sir ...'

Benik was already half out of his chair. 'What is it?'

'Leader Salamander is expected to arrive at the orbiter terminal in one hour, sir ...'

Benik snapped off the videophone so that the officer would not see his startled reaction to this surprising piece of information. Then a slow malicious smile spread gradually over his emaciated features. He rubbed his hands together with mounting excitement as he thought about the scoop he was going to achieve behind Donald Bruce's back. 'Poor old, Bruce. Odd how he always manages to be out of the way when there are big fish to be caught,' he muttered as he hurried out of the office.

When the Doctor and Giles Kent reached Melville after a hair-raising drive, Astrid introduced the Doctor to an astonished Fariah, who studied Salamander's double with fascinated disbelief. The Doctor's first concern was for news of Jamie and Victoria, and his kindly face hardened with worry as Astrid told him that they had almost certainly been caught and that they would probably be held in Europe by Salamander's security forces until he found time to deal with them.

'No, you're wrong,' Fariah butted in vehemently, 'Salamander doesn't care for loose ends. He'll bring them back here.'

The Doctor's face brightened with relief. 'To the Research Centre?' he asked hopefully.

Fariah nodded. 'Oh yes, Doctor. He will want to interrogate your two friends very thoroughly. He has all the necessary facilities at Kanowa.'

Again the Doctor' gentle face sank into deep furrows.

All this time Giles had been eyeing the black girl suspiciously. 'What the hell are *you* doing here anyway?' he demanded.

Fariah returned his gaze unflinchingly. It was clear that she disliked Kent, but she knew they had to work together now.

'Yes, young lady, I gather you work very closely with our Salamander friend,' the Doctor said suddenly, turning sharply.

'I did work for him. I was forced to,' Fariah retorted, her eyes blazing with resentment.

Kent laughed harshly. 'Forced! Tell the Doctor what you had done.'

The Doctor put up his hands and shook his head mildly. 'Does it matter?' he said quietly. 'We are none of us perfect, Mr Kent.'

67

Fariah seemed to relax a little. 'Thank you, Doctor,' she murmured, almost managing to smile at him.

The Doctor studied her for a moment. 'Now you wish to betray your Leader, a man who blackmailed you. You want revenge.'

'I wish to expose a monstrous tyrant.'

'Well, you are certainly in a unique position to do so,' the Doctor replied thoughtfully, rubbing the side of his nose.

Fariah came over to the chair and crouched cat-like beside him. 'I needed real proof, Doctor. Without it I would have been wasting my time. Now I have what you want,' she announced. 'I have proof! It concerns Nicholas Fedorin.'

Astrid turned to the Doctor with a sceptical shrug. 'A pathetic embezzler and racketeer who committed suicide yesterday,' she explained.

Fariah reached into her white tunic and drew out a thick wad of papers. 'Fedorin was a petty crook. But what none of you realise is that Salamander engineered most of the frauds himself,' she cried, flourishing the documents, 'and here's the proof.'

Kent swung round on her. 'How did you get your hands on that?' he demanded.

Fariah explained how, while she was serving Salamander's supper the previous evening, she noticed that the clock in the Leader's room struck the wrong number of chimes on the hour. Salamander was well known for his obsession with punctuality and she had seen him fiddling with the clock earlier in the day. So when she found herself alone in the room clearing away some time later, she had investigated, and the clockface had simply swung forward in her hands, revealing the wall-safe behind it.

The Doctor jumped to his feet, his face filled with admiration. 'Excellent work, my dear!' he cried, eagerly stretching out his hands for the file. 'At last. Evidence.'

Outside, Benik's security forces were silently taking up positions all round the building which, apart from Kent's office, was still empty for the New Year holiday. Armed men were concealed in the surrounding gardens, on the fire escapes and even on the roof by the time Benik's turbocar whined to a halt some distance away. He went straight to the courtyard, where he found their Lieutenant crouching in some huge ferns around an ornamental fountain, muttering urgently into his walkie-talkie.

'Just sealing up the gaps, sir,' he said, as Benik dropped down beside him. 'There are four of them in there now, on the third floor.'

Benik's eyes widened and he stared hungrily up at the third-floor windows as he sensed the chance to trap a nest of conspirators red-handed and so impress Salamander on his return.

A garbled message suddenly crackled from the radio. 'Ready now!' the Lieutenant muttered.

'If anyone makes a break for it, order your men to shoot on sight,' Benik instructed him coldly.

The Lieutenant looked appalled. 'But I can't take that responsibility, sir,' he protested. 'If the Zone police ...'

'You'll lose *all* responsbilities if you fail to obey!' Benik snarled. 'Those people are terrorists. Give the order.'

Reluctantly the officer obeyed, speaking rapidly into his radio.

Benik stood up, his eyes bright with the prospect of a coup. 'Now,' he breathed, leading the way into the silent building.

6

The Secret Empire

Upstairs Giles Kent was crouched down by the window and was peering intently over the sill. 'Come and look at this little lot,' he muttered.

The others joined him. Below them the security forces were closing in on the building.

'Benik's bully boys. We were followed,' Giles snapped.

He turned to the Doctor, but the Doctor had already read Kent's thoughts. He shook his head vehemently. 'No, Kent. I haven't time to prepare myself. We must find a way out of here,' he cried, furious at his own helplessness.

'Quick. The fire escape,' Astrid cried. But craning her head to look along the outside wall, she saw three or four guards already perched on the iron staircase. 'Too late. They've cornered us.'

At that moment the thud of boots came from the lobby. Giles rushed across and locked the outer door. For a second or two nobody moved.

'What can we do now?' Fariah murmured.

Suddenly the Doctor strode to the inner office door and yanked it open. 'Kent, I remember there's a kind of service panel in here.'

Giles struck himself on the forehead with his fist. 'Main air-conditioning duct. Of course. But it's three floors. Quite a drop,' he warned, hurrying over.

Just then there was a violent hammering on the outer

office door. 'Kent, you're completely surrounded,' Benik's voice shouted from the lobby. 'Let us in. It will save so much unpleasantness.'

The Doctor had found the jewelled clasp from his Salamander disguise in one of his pockets and was frantically using it to try and unscrew the large metal panel set into the wall of the inner office. As he worked, the onslaught on the outer door increased as Benik's guards started laying into it with their rifle butts. 'We'll just have to hope for a soft landing, my friends,' he muttered, grimacing with the effort of turning the tightly secured fixings, while the others watched anxiously over his shoulder.

'You cannot possibly escape!' Benik screamed at them. 'This is your last chance to give yourselves up.'

At last the Doctor managed to pull the panel free. 'Use your arms and legs against the sides of the duct and it should break your fall,' he whispered, motioning Fariah to go first.

'The file!' she gasped, diving back into the office to retrieve the precious papers.

Astrid urged the Doctor and Giles to go first. 'You are both more important,' she insisted, taking out her pistol.

The Doctor squeezed her hand encouragingly and clambered into the duct. He disappeared from sight, his hands and boots squeaking against the metal sides as he slid rapidly downwards. Taking a deep breath, Kent followed, then Fariah with the rolled up papers gripped between her teeth.

Astrid ran back into the main office and trained her gun on the door into the lobby. 'Get away from that door, Benik!' she shouted. Another barrage of rifle butts thundered against the thick hardwood. Astrid fired a short burst high up near the frame, and the attack on the door immediately stopped amid shouts of warning as the guards took cover. Astrid glanced at her watch, estimating how much of a start to give the others before she followed them into the duct. Then she raced into the inner office and scrambled into the duct just as a second burst of gunfire blew the locks off the outer door. It flew apart in a hail of splinters as three guards followed by Theodore Benik thrust their way in. They found the room deserted.

As Benik stared around him, his astonishment gave way to white hot rage at being cheated of his prey. He rushed into the inner office. 'The air ducts!' he fumed, hurling the metal panel aside. 'Alert the men outside. Tell them to shoot on sight.'

As the officer muttered orders into his radio, Benik rubbed his hands together with relish. 'They will be trapped in the air-conditioning plant perhaps. It's a muggy day and I think we should turn it on.'

Her hands and knees raw and burning from rubbing against the welded sections of the duct, Fariah forced herself through the narrow opening into the daylight. There was no sign of the Doctor or of Giles Kent in the deserted yard behind the building.

With cat-like stealth, Fariah ran along by the wall. Turning a corner, she saw Kent's motor caravan parked among some trees. She waved frantically and called out as she saw Giles scrambling into the driving seat. Simultaneously there was a crackle of shots behind her. A series of bright red holes exploded across the back of her white tunic and she was hurled against the wall. A security guard ran up and stood over her writhing body with his pistol levelled. The Lieutenant reached them a few seconds later, just as Kent's caravan roared away through the trees.

'Idiot!' he shouted. 'What do you think you're doing?'

The guard prodded the bloodstained girl at his feet. 'You gave orders to kill, sir.'

The Lieutenant shoved him aside. 'Go and report to Mr Benik that you carried out his orders and consequently allowed the most important suspects to escape!' he rapped, with a glare of contempt.

As the puzzled guard stamped away, the Lieutenant knelt down and tried to sit Fariah up. Her eyes flickered open and she clutched at her side with a desperate moan as Fedorin's bloodstained papers dropped out of her tunic.

'I'm sorry. You should have stopped running,' the officer murmured gently, supporting her as she fought for breath.

A moment later, Benik arrived. 'You lost them!' he snarled.

The shadow of a smile passed over Fariah's anguished face. Benik crouched over her, thrusting his pistol brutally against her forehead. 'Who is the other man with Kent and the Ferrier girl?' he demanded, elbowing the Lieutenant out of the way.

Again Fariah tried to smile. 'You ... you'll know soon enough,' she gasped.

'Who is he?' Benik screamed, shaking the dying girl by the hair. Fariah's body arched in agony and the Lieutenant protested to Benik in a shocked voice. 'Shut up,' Benik snapped. He twisted Fariah's curly black hair in his thin claw-like hand. 'Who is the stranger?' he repeated, shaking with rage. Then he pressed the barrel of his pistol between her eyes.

'You can't threaten ... me, Benik ... I can only die once ... and someone's beaten you ... to it ...' she whispered.

As Benik's finger squeezed the trigger, the officer pushed the gun aside. 'Sir! She's dead!' he cried.

The shot ripped harmlessly into the ground beside her head.

Wiping the sweat from his eyes with a vicious slash of his sleeve, Benik thrust his pistol into his tunic and gathered up the bloodstained papers scattered beside Fariah's motionless body. As he glanced quickly through them, a cunning smile began to creep over his thin, glistening face.

Two hours later Benik walked smugly through the heavy metal-alloy doors into Salamander's Sanctum in the heart of the Kanowa Research Centre. The armoured walls of the large, softly lit chamber were lined with orderly racks of documents, cassettes, microfilms and computer spools. In the centre was an extensive semi-circular console containing videophone, telex machines, television monitors and a vast array of electronic instruments. Salamander himself was sitting in a comfortable reclining chair behind the console talking to Donald Bruce who was facing him with his back to the doors.

'I always said we should finish Kent once and for all,' Benik said sharply as he entered, carrying the blood-spattered documents under his arm.

Bruce's bulky figure stiffened. 'What you mean is that you've failed miserably,' he said acidly, without turning round.

'A fiasco, Benik,' Salamander crowed in his menacing tenor, 'in public and in broad daylight.'

Bruce sighed and shook his head. 'You've exceeded your authority, Benik. A woman's been killed.'

'Resisting arrest,' Benik retorted.

The Security Commissioner's bushy eyebrows shot up. 'Arrest?' he echoed incredulously. 'Outside the Research Station perimeter you have no powers whatsoever. It was a gross violation.' He turned to Salamander, flushed with rage. 'This was a matter for the WZO!' he protested.

Benik sniggered insolently. 'Don't worry, Bruce. There was no one about in Melville today. You won't get any bad publicity.'

Salamander rapped sharply on the console with his fist. 'Kent and his associates are a menace to security,' he reminded them coldly. 'What action are you taking?'

Bruce shrugged. 'He hasn't broken any laws that I know of.'

Salamander laughed. 'Always the policeman, are you not Bruce?' He leaned towards them, an obsessive gleam in his dark eyes. 'Kent is known to associate with this stranger who impersonates me,' he murmured. 'The dangers are obvious. If they got in here, they could ruin everything. They must be found quickly. The safety of the Sunstore system may be at stake.' He paused significantly.

Donald Bruce grunted in agreement. 'Leave it to me,' he said briskly. Then he turned to Benik and beckoned him to follow. 'I'll review your internal security arrangements for a start.'

Benik did not move. He eyed Bruce with burning resentment and slowly held up the documents from Fedorin's file. 'This was found on the dead girl.'

Immediately Bruce put out his hand to take the papers, but Benik turned abruptly away and handed them to Salamander with a challenging stare in his saucer-like eyes.

Salamander recognised them at once. 'Excellent, Benik, excellent!' he exclaimed, pretending to glance through them.

Bruce cleared his throat deliberately. 'What is that?' he inquired with a suspicious frown. 'Any material evidence must ...'

'Top-security technical data,' Salamander hastily interrupted him, slipping the papers quickly into a drawer beside his chair. 'The Deputy Director has performed a remarkable service to the Centre by recovering it intact. Thank you, Benik.'

Bruce glared and then stamped out of the Sanctum. Benik gave Salamander a knowing smile and then followed him.

As soon as they had gone, Salamander muttered some terse instructions into the intercom in front of him. 'I am not to be disturbed until further notice. I shall engage the electro locks now.' He took a small electronic key from his jacket and inserted it into a series of small sockets set into one of the panels of instruments ranged along the angled front of the console. A few seconds later there was a succession of soft whirring and clicking sounds as the heavy doors were electronically sealed.

Sighing with satisfaction, Salamander swivelled his chair and busied himself at another panel. He adjusted its cluster of switches and touch-buttons, inserted the key into another socket and behind him a section of the wall swung smoothly open, revealing a kind of cylindrical capsule with a curved transparent shield over the front. Behind the shield hung a plastic radiation suit and helmet.

Salamander opened the shield with the key, took down the protective suit and hurriedly pulled it on over his clothes. Stepping into the capsule, he closed the shield over himself and inserted the key into the control panel in the wall of the cylinder. Immediately the capsule began to glide smoothly downwards inside its slim shaft.

Donald Bruce stood in the security control room of the Research Centre shaking his head in amazement.

'You're telling me that Salamander has shut himself away in that Sanctum of his and that he can't be reached?' he exclaimed.

The Duty Officer nodded. 'Correct, sir. All locks and communications are controlled from inside.'

'It's absurd!' Bruce cried. 'Suppose there's an emergency; how do you make contact?'

'The Kanowa Centre does not have emergencies,' Benik retorted with staggering complacency.

Bruce stared at the large, detailed plan of the Centre displayed on the wall. 'What goes on in this Sanctum anyway?'

Benik gestured at the plan. 'Classified area. I can only tell you that the Leader often works there in total isolation. No one gets in.'

Donald Bruce lost his temper. 'Suppose I ordered you to let me in there—in an emergency?' he thundered.

Benik shrugged. 'Really, Bruce, you charge in here like a bull in a china shop. But you won't get into the Sanctum. The electronic locks, once they're engaged, only open from the inside.'

The Security Commissioner looked long and hard at

Benik through his small wire-rimmed spectacles. 'I don't like mysteries,' he said frostily, 'any more than I like people trespassing on my territory.'

Benik smiled blandly. 'Then I suggest you get back to your 'territory' and find out what's happening, before Kent and his gang make a complete fool of you, in your absence,' he retorted and walked quickly out.

When the capsule came to rest sixty metres beneath the Sanctum, Salamander stepped out into the quietly humming underground Control Suite.

'The return of the hero to his grateful people,' he breathed, staring through a one-way window into a large cavernous laboratory hewn out of the rock. Gigantic machines resembling electromagnetic coils were positioned around the walls, interconnected by translucent coiled tubes along which pulses of strange phosphorescent light travelled in rhythmic bursts. Dozens of people in white overalls were stationed at the scattered panels, observing banks of instruments and making adjustments to their controls with zombie-like concentration.

In the centre of the chamber two men and a girl were deep in conversation. Salamander watched them carefully for a few moments as they pored over technical data sheets, totally engrossed in their work. Then he switched on the intercom on the console beside him.

Everyone down in the laboratory looked up expectantly as Salamander's voice suddenly boomed over the loudspeakers. 'Salamander to Mr Swann. Report to Control Suite. Observe radiation precautions.'

'He's done it. He's got back!' said the girl in a hushed, almost reverent, voice.

'Let's hope he brings better news this time, Mary,'

the young man said bleakly. 'Our stocks are almost exhausted.'

The elder man, Swann, nodded gravely. 'We can't go on much longer like this,' he murmured, fingering his thin gray moustache as he walked briskly away towards the steel staircase leading up into the Control Suite.

Mary moved closer to the young man. 'Are you going to ask Salamander, Colin?' she whispered.

'You bet I am. And he'll take me next time.'

Mary glanced furtively round to make sure they were not being overhead. 'I've had so many nightmares about you going up there, to the surface, Colin. None of the others he took ever came back.'

Colin Redmayne held Mary's arm. 'Don't try to stop me now,' he said fiercely. 'I've just got to get up there. I've got to walk on the earth again, see the sun again, no matter how dangerous it is.'

When Swann was let into the Control Suite, he found Salamander leaning weakly against the console, enclosed in the protective suit.

He hurried forward, forgetting all precautions. 'Are you all right, Leader?' he asked anxiously.

Salamander put up a warning hand. 'Do not approach, my friend. I have not yet decontaminated.' His voice was slurred and faint behind the mask and his eyes were rolling drunkenly. 'Too tired ... too ...'

'You must be more careful, you overexert yourself,' Swann murmured, his eyes full of concern. 'This repeated exposure is slowly destroying you.'

Salamander shrugged and forced a ghostly smile as he took off the helmet. 'But my people must eat. I am responsible for you all. What would you all do without me, Swann?'

He broke off dramatically and dragged himself across to a glass booth built into a corner of the chamber. As he entered it, he was bathed in a weird pinkish light. A series of red numbers flickered onto the liquid crystal display set into the wall. Gradually the numbers decreased, changed to green and then finally reached a steady value. The pinkish light faded and disappeared.

Swann stared apprehensively at the final reading as it blinked up on the indicator panel. 'Exposure level increases a little more each time, Leader,' he reported in a hushed voice.

Colin Redmayne had slipped into the Control Suite and was hovering diffidently by the door leading to the laboratory.

'One day I shall return from up there and the reading will remain in the red,' Salamander murmured, with a smile of resignation at the glimmering green digits. As he struggled painfully out of the decontamination booth, he caught sight of Colin's shocked face. 'Oh, I joke, just to frighten you a little,' he added with a tired laugh. 'But I have such news for you all ...'

'We can go back! We can return to the surface!' Colin cried, eagerly coming forward. Behind him Mary Smith had appeared in the doorway too.

'Not so fast my children, not so fast,' Salamander said, speaking with difficulty again. 'It is not yet safe for you. But I want you to know that I have discovered more food supplies. They are not contaminated. They will give us more time.' Salamander almost stumbled and he clutched hold of Swann's arm for support.

Swann gestured angrily to the two young technicians to leave the Control Suite at once.

As they quietly obeyed, Salamander called bravely after them, 'Celebrate this great discovery among yourselves. Open some wine and drink to the future.'

Swann operated the electronic door from the console and it slid shut behind them. Then he watched as Salamander began to struggle feebly out of the protective suit, fumbling like a child. 'Leader, you should rest,' Swann urged him.

Salamander shook his head. 'But there is so much to be done first.' Nevertheless, he allowed Swann to help him over to a comfortable couch in an alcove, where he lay down and immediately closed his eyes. Swann lingered a moment, wondering whether to finish removing the radiation suit, or to creep quietly away. Then he dimmed the lights and crept back to the laboratory. When he had gone, Salamander opened his eyes and lay there in the eerie glow from the console instruments, his body shaking with silent laughter.

The rare sound of laughter and of eager chatter filled the laboratory some time later. Colin and Mary had opened a flagon of wine and were handing out plastic beakers half-filled with an oily, yellowish liquid. Nobody seemed to mind the coarse sulphury taste, as the technicians gathered in small groups where they could still keep an eye on their instruments, and gratefully sipped the crude but highly alcoholic concoction.

A sudden cheer went up as Salamander appeared unexpectedly at the top of the stairs to the Control Suite. He had taken off the radiation suit and he spread his arms in greeting to the throng below.

Swann hurried up to the Leader and handed him a

full beaker of wine before raising his own almost empty one high in the air. 'To a great and humane man!' he cried.

The toast was heartily echoed around the chamber and everyone drank.

Salamander raised his brimming beaker, shaking his head modestly. 'Please, please, my friends, it is joy and honour enough to have returned safely among you,' he cried. 'In a few weeks it will be five long years that we have all survived here in this shelter together, survived and worked together towards a new future.' He paused impressively for several seconds.

In the sudden silence all eyes were fixed on the Leader as he handed his untasted drink to Swann. Salamander swept his audience with a triumphant smile. 'You are the brave guardians of true freedom,' he told them. 'Your tireless work down here creates natural disasters wherever the enemies of freedom and truth persist in their insane and poisonous wars up there on the surface. And so we enable our beloved planet to fight her enemies in her own way, by the laws of Nature and not those of the sword and the missile. Our most recent attack, in the Eperjest Tokyar region, has been a complete success. All missile silos have been destroyed and the forces of tyranny there are defeated for ever.'

Enthusuastic applause burst out as the Leader turned to re-enter the Control Suite, but a lone voice suddenly rose above the appreciative clamour. It was Colin Redmayne's.

'When, Leader? When?' he cried, his pale face now flushed and his eyes bright. 'Tell us when we can return to the sun and the daylight again.'

There was a sudden silence as Salamander stared out over the sea of shocked faces and studied the young man who had dared to challenge him. 'When the poisoned atmosphere is clean, when the senseless war is over and the hate is all destroyed,' he declared, gesturing wearily up at the roof of the cavern. 'Until then you must have patience.'

Colin ran to the bottom of the staircase. 'Always the same speech,' he cried recklessly, 'but we have to live this nightmare every day, until none of us can remember what a day is any more.' Colin's eyes were filled with a wild and passionate fire as he gazed up at the Leader. 'I want to escape. I want to go up there and see for myself,' he cried.

'You will, you will, Colin,' Salamander promised. 'You must all have faith. You must all trust me. I cannot allow you to leave here until I know it is safe. We must all fight on.'

Then he disappeared into the Control Suite and the heavy door slid shut. Salamander lounged back in the luxurious chair facing his console, a fat cigar clamped in his mouth and a large lavishly illustrated book on butterflies spread open across his knees. He studied the book with intense interest, occasionally glancing at the scene through the one-way window and muttering an encouraging acknowledgement to Swann's communications on the intercom. 'Excellent, Swann, excellent. Keep them on their toes.'

7

A Scrap of Truth

After a hair-raising journey along dusty, pot-holed tracks avoiding the main highways, Giles Kent had driven his caravan into a deep wooded ravine only three kilometres from the Kanowa Research Centre perimeter. It was parked among trees and dense undergrowth just off a tortuous dirt road which ran between steep scrub-covered slopes.

Inside, the Doctor was sitting with a towel round his shoulders while Astrid was busy styling his hair and eyebrows with frequent glances at a photograph of Salamander which Giles held up for her. The Doctor looked miserable and he kept fidgeting irritably so that Astrid had to ask him repeatedly to sit still and concentrate. He had been brooding over Fariah's disappearance ever since their escape from Melville.

'I just cannot understand how we lost her. She was right behind me,' he murmured, carefully watching Kent's reflection.

Kent had witnessed Fariah's fate but he had kept quiet, fearing that the Doctor would have insisted on trying to rescue her. 'I told you. She must have got stuck in the ducts,' he said. 'Stop worrying, Doctor. She'll turn up. She's a clever girl'

To Astrid's dismay the Doctor shook his head angrily. 'You don't seem to appreciate how vital she is,' he cried. 'She has Fedorin's file, she has been one of

Salamander's closest associates and she is herself one of his blackmail victims. For what it's worth, that young lady is our evidence at the moment.' As he spoke, the Doctor again looked hard at the wiry Australian reflected in the mirror. There seemed to be something odd about the man, but still the Doctor could not fathom it. Suddenly the door flew open and a WZO policeman armed with a machine pistol leaped into the caravan. Behind him came Donald Bruce.

'And you, sir, are *my* evidence!' he boomed, pointing to the startled Doctor with a satisfied smile. Kent stared at Bruce in sullen disbelief. 'How did you know we were here?' he demanded.

The Security Commissioner took a small metallic disc from his pocket. 'Your last visitor took the sensible precaution of attaching this to your chassis,' he explained.

The Doctor cast his eyes to the roof. 'Mr Benik,' he muttered. 'A neat little micropulse transmitter.' He was furious with himself for not having suspected such a trick earlier. 'So you've been following us.'

But Donald Bruce was not listening. He was gazing down at the Doctor in fascination. 'It's quite incredible,' he exclaimed. 'If you were to stand face to face, Salamander would think he was looking in a mirror. No wonder you fooled me last time we met. Who are you?'

The Doctor smiled wearily. 'If you had two or three years to spare I could tell you. Just think of me as the Doctor.'

'So. How much are they paying you, Doctor?' Bruce demanded with a contemptuous nod at the others.

The Doctor rose to his feet indignantly. 'I beg your pardon?' he cried.

'To impersonate Salamander, so that they can

85

destroy him and put you in his place.'

'I could not possibly be a party to any such plan,' the Doctor protested. 'The fact is that Salamander is quite illegally holding prisoner two young friends of mine. I am merely attempting to arrange for their release.'

Astrid stepped forward defiantly. 'And also to gather evidence which will expose Salamander for what he really is: a blackmailer, a murderer and a tyrant,' she said vehemently.

Bruce stared at her as if she were mad. 'An ambitious little scheme, Miss Ferrier. How do you know such evidence exists?'

Giles Kent moved in sharply. 'It's all there in the Research Centre,' he said, 'in Salamander's Sanctum. No doubt someone like you can get in there any time he wants.' Kent knew that this last remark would touch a sore spot.

Bruce said nothing for a while, but stood there frowning at Kent and running over in his mind the curious facts he had discovered about security arrangements at Kanowa.

The Doctor broke the silence. 'We do possess a piece of undeniable evidence suggesting that Salamander is not quite so pure and white as he might like us to believe.

Bruce glanced sharply at him. 'What is that?' he asked almost eagerly.

The Doctor told Bruce about the Fedorin file and the coincidence of Fedorin's recent death.

'Show me this file!' Bruce said excitedly when the Doctor had finished.

'Fariah Neguib has it,' Astrid informed him.

'But she's dead. Shot while resisting arrest,' Bruce told them.

Kent shook his head. 'Gunned down illegally by Benik's mob because she was a threat to Salamander,' he shouted angrily.

Bruce blinked uncertainly behind his spectacles.

The Doctor looked appalled. 'This is terrible news ... an innocent girl ...' He glanced agitatedly around at the others. 'No doubt Benik has found the file and will return it to Salamander.'

Astrid moved for the door, but was stopped by the police officer. 'If he does, we have no hope of pressing our case against Salamander. We've got to stop him!' she cried.

'Stay where you are!' Bruce snapped. He looked at the three suspects for a moment, thinking back over the incident in the Sanctum with Benik and the documents Salamander had refused to show him.

'As it happens I am not entirely satisfied with some aspects of the way Salamander runs his organisation,' he admitted. 'However, I shall investigate in my own way.'

There was a sudden blur of activity as Astrid grabbed the barrel of the policeman's pistol and gave it a sharp twist, throwing the unsuspecting officer flat on his face. Before Bruce could do anything, she had him covered.

'As head of world security, Mr Bruce, you really should be better protected,' she said, with a mocking smile.

'But you're completely surrounded, you know,' Bruce laughed patronisingly. 'You surely don't imagine I came here with just one man?'

Astrid seemed not to hear. Her eyes were bright with purpose. 'You're not going to stop us now we've got this far.'

The Doctor held out his hand. 'May I, Miss Ferrier?'

he requested gently, bowing his head slightly but keeping his eyes level.

Astrid glanced from the Doctor to the pistol she was holding and back again with a baffled frown.

'Please. You can trust me,' the Doctor reassured her, taking the gun from her hands, which seemed to make no effort to resist, his eyes fixing hers with a Salamander-like stare.

The others watched in confusion as he pushed the barrel into Donald Bruce's ribs. 'Now, Mr Bruce. You admit that at this moment your life is in my hands?' he murmured.

Bruce said nothing, but licked his dry lips, watching the Doctor like a hawk. There was a long silence.

Then the Doctor suddenly turned the pistol round and offered the butt to Bruce with a smile.

Both Giles and Astrid uttered incredulous gasps and lunged forward to seize the pistol. But Bruce beat them to it. Snatching the gun, he waved it at them at point-blank range.

'What the hell have you done?' Kent exploded, grabbing the Doctor's arm.

'You fool!' Astrid spat at him. 'You fool!'

The Doctor shook his head, with an enigmatic smile. 'Don't worry my friends. Mr Bruce is not going to shoot us, are you, Bruce?'

The air was electric with tension and uncertainty as Giles and Astrid glanced from the Doctor to Donald Bruce, trying to fathom what was going on.

At last Bruce broke the silence. 'Why did you do that?'

'Because I think you are an honest and reasonable man,' the Doctor replied simply. 'Because I trust you and I want you to trust me.'

Bruce studied him for a while. 'What do you expect to gain from this ... this gesture?' he asked.

'Your confidence and your cooperation, Mr Bruce.'

Giles and Astrid exchanged despairing glances. It was almost as if Salamander himself were standing there and calmly wrecking their plans in front of their eyes.

'You propose that I investigate Kent's accusations against the Leader by helping you to get into the Centre disguised as Salamander,' he said slowly, as if he were reading a description of the fantastic scheme out of a book.

The Doctor nodded eagerly.

Bruce considered for a moment. 'And what if there is no evidence to substantiate these charges?' he asked.

'Then you will be free to arrest us,' the Doctor replied. 'And to send us for trial, naturally,' he added.

Bruce glanced doubtfully at Giles and at Astrid. Then he suddenly seemed to shake his bulky frame into action. 'Very well, Doctor, but on one condition,' he agreed. 'Kent and Miss Ferrier stay here as hostages. You and I go alone.'

As the Doctor nodded his assent, Giles erupted violently. 'Now wait!' he shouted. 'I'm not going to be held as any hostage. I must go with you.'

'Otherwise it's no deal,' Astrid added vehemently.

The Doctor raised his hands and bowed his head in an appeal for calm. He turned to Giles and Astrid. 'If I am going to undertake this task, you must cooperate with Mr Bruce,' he told them firmly.

Bruce handed the pistol to his officer, who had observed everything in total confusion. 'Watch them,' he ordered. 'But if they know what's good for them, they shouldn't cause you any trouble.'

The two hostages watched in sullen silence as the Doctor gave his hair a final sleek behind his ears. He fished around in his pockets for his clasp and pinned it in place under his chin. Then he buttoned the jacket they had found for him and spent a few seconds choosing some rings from a box of old theatrical jewellery on the table.

Finally he turned to Giles and Astrid and said in his chilling Salamander voice, 'Remain here until I return, my friends, and all will be well.' He grimaced like a melodrama villain and waggled his beringed fingers at them mischievously.

They stared impassively back at the clowning figure, while the police officer looked stunned. Donald Bruce shook his head in admiration. 'I must be out of my mind to trust you,' he muttered. 'I only hope you can fool Benik with this caper. If he sees through you, then we're all of us finished ...'

Meanwhile, sixty metres beneath the Kanowa Research Centre the capsule slid gently down to rest at the bottom of its shaft. Salamander opened the transparent shield and stepped out into the quietly humming Control Suite. This time he had not bothered to wear the protective suit. He went straight to the observation window and made an announcement on the tannoy.

'Salamander to Swann. I have returned. Routine radiation precautions are in force. Fresh supplies are coming down on the conveyor. Detail personnel to unload and then report progress on schedule seven.'

Swann selected several technicians and led them over to a large perspex-fronted hatch set into the rocky wall of the chamber. They pulled on thick protective gloves

90

and waited, watching the liquid crystal digital display fitted beside the hatch, as a large packing-case slowly descended into the bay behind the shield. A buzzer sounded and the radiation counter flickered up a series of red numbers. A pinkish glow filled the bay and after a while the numbers blinked into green and the glow faded.

Swann watched while the technicians opened the hatch, manhandled the crate onto a low trolley and then closed the shield again to wait for the next consignment. Then he walked briskly through the chamber, stopping at various sections to make checks and collect data on schedule seven.

When he reached Colin Redmayne and Mary Smith's section, Colin seized his arm and pulled him close so that he could whisper in his ear. 'Swann, have you ever wondered what would happen if Salamander failed to come back one day?' he muttered furtively.

Swann ran his practised eye over their data print-outs. 'I've warned you about this kind of subversive talk, Redmayne,' he murmured. 'It isn't healthy.'

When Swann had moved on, Colin leaned on the instrument panel, head in hands. 'That's right. Don't think. Just work. Eat—when there's enough to go round. Sleep. Blind worms under the earth, wriggling without purpose,' he murmured savagely.

Mary moved beside him. 'Swann daren't let people think, Colin,' she said quietly. 'If he did, then they'd begin to …'

'That is the beginning of the end,' he retorted. He thumped the computer console. 'What *is* all this? What are we doing down here? I have to go. To see for myself, Mary. And I will,' he breathed.

Swann had stopped by the conveyor hatch and was running his eye over the growing stack of crates on the trolley. Noticing a scrap of paper sticking out from under one of the smaller cases, he bent down and pulled it out. He was about to screw it up and toss it into a nearby disposal shute when something caught his eye and made him look again. He remained a long time staring at it, his eyes repeatedly going out of focus and looking through the faded words and then focussing on them again.

Eventually Swann began to wander slowly towards the staircase in the corner of the laboratory. As he passed her, Mary Smith reported that her section was now back to normal operating power, but Swann walked by without a word, like a sleepwalker, bumping into people and equipment, and ignoring questions.

Salamander released the electric locks and Swann walked into the Control Suite.

'Thank you, Mr Swann. Just leave the data there. I shall run through it later,' Salamander murmured without looking up.

Swann let the heavy clipboard fall onto the console with a crash and stood there silently.

Salamander stiffened and glanced sharply up at him. 'Is something wrong, Mr Swann?' he exclaimed, a diamond-hard edge in his voice.

'What ... what's this ... this ...' Swann whispered almost inaudibly, the damp piece of newspaper lying limply in his hands. 'Look at the *date*!' His voice had abruptly changed to a shrill scream. He was trembling violently and the scrap of newspaper was already beginning to disintegrate in his feverish grasp. 'North American Zone Bulletin,' he shrieked, 'dated not two months ago. And it says ... it says ...'

Salamander took the flimsy scrap of paper and stared at the blurred headline. FREAK TIDAL WAVE SINKS CARIBBEAN CRUISEFOIL: 500 VACATIONERS MISSING.

'Just a few weeks ago, a cruise ship full of holiday-makers,' Swann cried frenziedly. 'How, Salamander? How? What about the radiation, the poisoned air, the devastation? What about the war?'

Keeping his shocked and worried face averted, Salamander desperately tried to think, while Swann followed him about, babbling hysterically. 'Lies. Just lies. You've kept us all down here and deceived us all these years. Why. What for?'

'I had to Swann!' Salamander suddenly cried, turning on him violently. 'It was necessary.'

Swann stared at him incredulously. 'But *why*?' he breathed.

Salamander shuddered and passed his hand across his eyes. 'The war is over up there, that is true,' he said wearily. 'But have you any idea what happens to people in chemical and nuclear warfare, Swann?'

'How could I?' Swann shouted. 'I've been down here in this damned cage!'

'The survivors are eaten away in body and in mind, Swann. They have a kind of society, but corrupt and violent. The normal human values are destroyed. Members of the same family kill one another for food.'

'But that report ... the holiday cruise in the Caribbean ...'

'Propaganda,' Salamander shrugged. 'A subtle attempt to persuade the survivors that their tyrannical rulers are succeeding in building a normal world again. But it is a jungle of nightmares up there, Swann. Do you imagine I could ever allow you all to be exposed to its evils?'

Swann slowly sat down. He seemed to have grown calmer as he listened to Salamander's horrific description of the world above them.

'You could have told me at least,' he said quietly when Salamander had finished.

'It has been hard to bear such a secret, Swann. But I dare not take the risk of jeopardising our work here.'

Swann pondered a moment. 'Our work here,' he murmured at last. 'The volcanoes, the earthquakes, the floods—what is the purpose of all this?'

Salamander sat down opposite him and looked earnestly into his eyes. 'To eliminate the sick and perverted rabble that have survived the holocaust up there. I wish for you and the others, all of us here, to inherit the Earth and create a new world, Swann,' he said fervently.

'But that's murder. It's genocide!' Swann cried, horrified.

'No, it is an act of mercy. I promise you.'

Swann was silent for a while. Then he rose and stood over Salamander. 'Your promises are no longer enough. I want to see for myself.'

Slowly Salamander got to his feet. 'My friend, you will not survive the horror, the sudden exposure to radiation. It is terribly dangerous.'

But Swann stood his ground. 'Take me to the surface, or I shall reveal what you have told me to the others,' he retorted.

Salamander was disconcerted by the sudden strength in Swann's manner. He looked at his chief technician for some time, while a plan formed in the dark recesses of his mind.

Eventually he nodded. 'Very well, Swann, I agree to your demand. But you do this at your own risk,' he said harshly. 'I cannot accept responsibility for your safety.'

8

Deceptions

Victoria regained consciousness first. Jamie came to on the stretcher beside hers with a parched groan. 'Where are we?' he croaked, staring round at the sinister pieces of apparatus lining the walls.

'You are in the Behaviour Analysis Unit of the Kanowa Research Centre,' Benik informed them as he hurried in, followed by an armed security guard, who closed the door and stood in front of it.

'Who are you?' Jamie asked disinterestedly.

'*I* ask the questions,' Benik said 'and I get all the answers I want.'

'Not from me you won't,' Jamie said, tottering to his feet.

Benik uttered a shriek of laughter. 'Good. Good, I like that. You have spirit, boy. That makes my task much more rewarding.' He gestured at the menacing devices surrounding them.

Jamie was hobbling painfully about as if something were wrong with his leg. Suddenly he straightened up, driving his fist into the guard's stomach like a steam-hammer. The guard crumpled in half and slumped to the floor. Jamie was about to seize the gun, when a terrified scream made him spin round. Benik had his arm round Victoria's neck and he was holding a pistol to her head. Her face was a mask of horror. For a second it looked as if Jamie intended to launch himself at her assailant, but he stopped himself and stood there helplessly, staring at Benik.

Benik ran the barrel of his pistol through Victoria's long, thick hair. 'Such pretty hair,' he breathed, his face glowing with sweat as he leaned closer and closer towards her pale cheek.

'All right,' Jamie gasped, unable to hold back any longer. 'Leave her alone. What do you want to know?'

Very slowly and deliberately, Benik twisted the pistol barrel tighter and tighter into Victoria's hair, not taking his eyes off Jamie's tortured face for a moment. 'Now, who put you up to all this nonsense. Giles Kent?' he demanded scornfully.

One glance at Victoria's face convinced Jamie that he had no choice but to talk—to tell Benik exactly what he wanted to hear. But as he opened his mouth to speak, Salamander walked into the room followed by Donald Bruce. They almost tripped over the semi-conscious guard lying across the threshold.

The Deputy swallowed his surprise in a flash and released Victoria with a furtive shove. 'I was not informed that you had left the Sanctum, Leader,' he muttered, glancing resentfully at Donald Bruce and then looking Salamander up and down with a puzzled frown.

'I had a shower and slipped into something more relaxing,' Salamander replied quickly, with a glare that put Benik firmly in his place. He turned and surveyed the prisoners with narrowed eyes, his white teeth flashing behind his curling lips. 'And what have they confessed to so far?'

Benik tried not to look at Bruce's grimly contemptuous face behind Salamander's back. 'Nothing yet, Leader,' he admitted at last.

'Nothing?' Salamander exclaimed. He waved Benik

away. 'You are wasting time. Bruce and I will take over.'

Benik stood motionless a moment, almost visibly curling up with disappointment. Then he thrust his pistol away and walked to the door.

'And take your puppy dog with you!' Salamander flung over his shoulder.

Benik helped the dazed guard to his feet. 'But Leader, you should have protection,' he protested.

The Security Commissioner shook his head and gave Benik a faint smile as he took out his own pistol and levelled it at the two prisoners.

When the white-faced Benik had dragged the stumbling guard out of the room, Salamander turned to Jamie. 'And now Señor McCrimmon ...'

'We've nothing to tell ye,' Jamie snapped defiantly, to Victoria's horror. She could not see how they could avoid a full confession now.

'Is that the way to greet an old friend,' the Doctor asked gently, his cynical smile changing abruptly into a mischievous grin.

The shock of hearing the Doctor's familiar voice and of seeing Salamander's cruel glint transformed as if by magic into the familiar impish twinkle, made Victoria jump back in alarm. Then she flung her arms round him and hugged him with affectionate relief. 'Doctor, you're a genius!' she cried, laughing.

Jamie thumped the Doctor heartily on the back, smiling with delight and shaking his head in admiration.

The Doctor wagged a cautionary finger and put on his Salamander expression. 'Take care, Lieutenant McCrimmon!' he snarled.

Donald Bruce had been watching these antics with an impatient frown. 'Doctor, this is getting us nowhere,' he complained.

The Doctor looked hurt. 'I do not agree. You must admit you've just witnessed most convincing proof of my ability to impersonate Salamander,' he retorted indignantly.

The World Security Commissioner nodded exasperatedly. 'Yes, yes, Doctor. But please do let' get on with what we came here to do. We don't have much time.'

At that moment Theodore Benik was storming into the Security Control Room on the other side of the Administration Block. 'Why was I not informed that the Leader had left the Sanctum?' he demanded, his eyes blazing at the duty officer.

The officer glanced at his security systems display. 'The Leader is still inside the Sanctum, sir. The electro-locks are still engaged,' he reported, looking puzzled.

'Impossible. You must have a fault here,' Benik snapped, leaning over and jabbing a series of touch-buttons.

The officer checked his display once more. 'I assure you that the Leader has not left the Sanctum, sir,' he insisted, turning to Benik almost apologetically.

But the Deputy Director had gone. He was hurrying along the anonymous concrete corridors towards the Sanctum. When he reached it, he tried the access switches. Nothing happened. He tried again. Still nothing. The heavy shutters remained sealed.

Benik turned and stared down the corridor in the direction of the Behaviour Analysis Unit where he had left Salamander not five minutes previously. Something odd was going on and Benik was determined to find out what it was.

Salamander stopped the capsule halfway up the shaft between the underground Control Suite and the Sanctum on the surface. Moving clumsily in his protective suit, he opened the shield and led Swann out into a steeply sloping tunnel dimly lit by a string of naked bulbs slung along the roof. A warm breeze blew down the roughly hewn tunnel, and Swann gazed along it expectantly.

'Where does it lead to?' he asked eagerly.

'Into a ruined building on the surface,' Salamander told him. 'I assemble the supplies up there and then they come down on the conveyor.'

'The surface!' Swann cried excitedly, starting to scramble hastily up the scree-strewn slope.

Salamander grabbed his arm. 'Wait. Not that way. This way is much safer,' he said soothingly, steering Swann towards a dark, narrow gully leading off the main tunnel opposite the capsule.

Swann allowed himself to be pushed through the niche into a deep, unlit cave scattered with splinters of rock and huge boulders. He stumbled uncertainly forward towards the slit of light ahead of them. A warm, sweet-scented wind suddenly flooded the gully and Swann soon found himself standing blinking in the strong sunlight at the entrance to the cave.

For several seconds he was speechless, shading his eyes and staring at the brilliant blue sky and at the bright leaves of the vegetation covering the slopes of the ravine below them.

Then he turned to his guide, his face alive with ecstasy. 'It's beautiful! It's so beautiful,' he murmured. 'I had almost forgotten. The sky ... the trees down there ...' He stared across at the miraculous panorama shimmering in the heat beyond the ravine. 'You could have brought the others this far, just to see,' he said quietly, his eyes lost in the landscape.

Behind him Salamander shook his head. 'You forget Swann, one or two did come in the past. But they succumbed to the contamination. Already you have been here too long without protection.'

Swann walked a few paces to the edge of the ravine as if mesmerised. 'But everything looks just as it used to,' he exclaimed. 'Where are the mutations you talked of. The sky is so clear. You spoke of the dust belts, the darkness at noon ...'

Unseen, Salamander had picked up a sharp sliver of flint. 'You are taking a terrible risk coming out here like this, my friend,' he murmured, raising the crude weapon high over the back of Swann's head. 'But I did my best to warn you.'

Just too late Swann turned, and the savage blow sliced into his skull, sending him reeling with his hair rapidly filling with blood. His piercing scream echoed through the cavern and the tunnel for several seconds as he fell back onto his back, staring up into the azure sky with the hot sun beating relentlessly into his strangely smiling face. Tears welled out of his eyes and ran, mingling with his blood, in streams onto the dry ground.

After a while his head moved slowly from side to side as his lips worked in agonised desperation to form words.

'Nothing ... ' he breathed hoarsely, his entire body shaken by convulsive sobs. 'Nothing's changed ... '

In the bottom of the ravine the WZO police officer guarding Giles Kent and Astrid Ferrier had taken up his position outside the motor caravan to give himself a better chance of stopping any surprise move by the two hostages. Inside, Giles was moving about agitatedly like a penned animal while Astrid watched him calmly.

'I have to get in there, Astrid!' he muttered. 'This is our one chance and we can't risk Bruce bungling things.'

Astrid shook her head firmly. 'No, Giles. We can't risk losing Bruce's confidence by breaking the agreement. At least he's agreed to investigate.'

Giles gave a short cynical laugh. 'That great elephant wouldn't recognise evidence if it was staring him in the face.' He seized Astrid by the shoulders and almost shook her. 'Look, if I was in there, I could lead them straight to the nitty gritty,' he said, his jaw clenched with frustration.

Astrid stared back at him impassively. Eventually she spoke. 'If I distracted the guard, it might give you say fifteen minutes to reach the fence,' she murmured.

Kent hugged her. 'Good girl. Just take care of our friend outside for a few minutes and leave the rest to me,' he said.

Astrid thought for a moment and then began rummaging among the remains of the provisions which still lay in a jumbled heap in the locker. 'I'm ready, Giles,' she said, brandishing a bottle of tomato ketchup which had survived the attack by Benik's guard earlier.

A few minutes afterwards Giles Kent was lying face down on one of the divans, his body spread-eagled and motionless. His hands and shirtsleeves were mottled with vivid red droplets.

Astrid leaned over him and smashed one of the windows with a sharp blow of the bottle. Then she let out a long, terrifying scream as she carefully replaced

101

the bottle in the locker. The caravan door was wrenched open and the police officer sprang inside, vizor down and machine pistol levelled. 'What happened?' the officer shouted, keeping his distance. 'What happened?'

Astrid pointed to the shattered window, gibbering and moaning hysterically, 'Shot ... someone shot ... through the window,' she stuttered.

The officer glanced up at the shattered pane and then cautiously approached the body, keeping his eyes and the gun on Astrid. He turned Kent over and winced at the large red stain covering the whole of the left side of Giles's shirt-front. The victim's staring eyes told him all he needed to know. Gently he lowered the body back onto the divan and watched the chest for a few seconds.

'Looks like he's a goner, but there might be a pulse,' he said, turning. 'If you've got a ...'

But the caravan was empty. Astrid had disappeared. Throwing himself through the doorway just in time to see something moving through the edge of the undergrowth, the officer fired several long bursts from his pistol. Then, with a vicious curse, he set off in pursuit, firing volley after volley as he scrambled through the dense foliage.

When it was quiet Giles leapt to his feet and quickly went to look outside. Wiping as much of the red sauce off his shirt as he could, he washed his hands and then pulled on his tunic, buttoning it to the throat to hide the stains. He picked up Astrid's bag and found her small automatic still inside it. Slipping it into his tunic, he went to the door and glanced around once again just to be sure.

With a smile of grim determination on his haggard face, he set off in the direction of the Kanowa Research Centre. He knew that time was desperately short and that he was about to take the biggest gamble of his life.

Astrid struggled up the scrub-covered hillside higher up the ravine, her lungs bursting and her throat feeling like sandpaper in the heat. She had taken care not to get too far ahead of her pursuer in case he gave up the chase and returned to the caravan before Giles could make his breakaway. She glanced at her watch. Ten minutes. Giles should have got the start he needed.

Above and to one side of her she saw the black slit of a narrow cave entrance. Dragging herself over the crumbling scree towards it, she suddenly heard a pitiful croaking voice crying out, 'Somebody, please ... please help me ...'

Reaching the cave, she found the crooked, writhing body of an elderly man dressed in blood-spattered white overalls trying to drag himself aimlessly across the baking hot ground. 'Who did this to you?' she whispered, shocked and angry.

Swann tried to speak, but no sound seemed to come. Astrid put her ear next to his swollen lips. 'Sal . . . a . . . mand . . .' he breathed. Swann clutched her arm and tried to turn his head towards the interior of the cave. 'There . . . in there . . .' he gasped faintly.

Astrid peered into the darkness. 'Salamander is in there?' she murmured doubtfully.

Swann nodded slowly with agonising moans. Suddenly he threw up his arms and tried to push her away from him. 'You ... you are danger ... radiation ...' he croaked, staring at her in frightened bewilderment, the sweat pouring down his filthy, bloodstained face.

As gently as she could, Astrid lifted him under the arms and pulled him into the shade. 'Don't be afraid.

I'm going to find water for you,' she murmured, knowing full well that there was no chance of finding any, nor of saving the mortally injured man.

'The others,' he cried. 'You must help the others ...'

'What others?' Astrid asked. 'I do want to help you. Just tell me.'

'You must bring them up,' Swann pleaded. 'Prisoners. Salamander kept us prisoners. Down there.' With a final surge of strength, Swann seized Astrid's sleeve. 'Swear it, please,' he cried, 'swear it.'

Swann's words echoed round the cave long after his body had slumped against her, dead. She felt for his pulse and then passed her hand over his hideously staring eyes to close them for ever, before gently laying him onto the rocky floor.

'I swear it,' she murmured. Tense with the conviction that she was about to discover the vital evidence against Salamander for which she and Giles had searched for so long, Astrid ventured cautiously into the enemy's secret empire underground ...

In the Behaviour Analysis Unit the Doctor was sitting hunched deep in thought on the edge of a bench. He had considered carefully all the information which Jamie and Victoria had just poured out concerning their experiences in the Central European Zone, and he had given his assessment of the evidence to Donald Bruce.

The Security Commissioner's simmering disbelief finally boiled over. 'Are you trying to tell me that Salamander has been attacking selected areas of the world by causing natural disasters artificially—and that he's been doing it from here?' he cried, controlling his urge to laugh in the Doctor's face. 'It's preposterous.'

'I believe it is quite possible, Bruce. If we can penetrate the Sanctum I think we shall find proof,' the Doctor replied, getting up and walking round the laboratory, whistling quietly to himself.

At that moment the door opened and Benik hurried in carrying a large sheaf of documents. Bruce immediately launched into a tough barrage of questions directed at Jamie and Victoria, as if he were in the middle of interrogating them.

'Yes? What is it Benik?' the Doctor rapped, in his Salamander voice.

'Supply requisitions, Leader,' Benik replied. 'Your approval and signature, please.'

The Doctor calmly took the documents and the pen from Benik and ran his eye over the requisitions. While he studied them, Benik informed him that there seemed to be a fault with the doors to the Sanctum.

'Get Maintenance to deal with it,' the Doctor snapped, without looking up.

'They are completely jammed, Leader. Maintenance will require your personal electrokey,' Benik persisted.

Bruce could not stop himself glancing anxiously round. The Doctor said nothing for a moment. Then he patted his tunic distractedly, still studying the documents Benik had handed him.

'Madness!' the Doctor exclaimed. 'I must have left the electrokey in the Sanctum. Tell Maintenance to do their best,' he ordered, 'and don't wait for these schedules now.'

Benik hesitated, then without another word, he turned and walked quickly out of the laboratory.

As soon as the door had shut, Jamie gave a low whistle. 'That was a wee bit close for comfort, Doctor,' he muttered.

'Benik may be on to us,' Donald Bruce warned them. 'I know that shrewd little worm only too well.'

The Doctor seemed not to hear them. He was scrutinising the sheaf of papers with intense concentration, muttering under his breath and shaking his head.

'Come and look at these statistics, Bruce!' he eventually cried. 'This is a real prize! Just look at these monthly provisions figures,' the Doctor pointed out. 'Enough for a community of at least a hundred people. How many personnel are there in this place?'

Bruce considered for a moment. 'I'd reckon around fifty all told. But many of them live outside the Centre.' With a puzzled frown, Bruce looked more closely at the figures.

The Doctor flicked through the pages. 'And these equipment orders,' he mused, his hands trembling with excitement. 'Sonar flux intensifiers, magnetic field filtering prisms—nothing to do with any solar-collecting systems *I've* ever come across, Bruce. But a very useful set of spares for some kind of apparatus designed to cause highly selective and localised earth tremors and assorted geophysical firework displays.'

'Earthquakes and volcanoes,' Bruce murmured after a lengthy pause.

The Doctor nodded vigorously, thrusting the papers into Bruce's large, fleshy hands. 'Hang on to these, Bruce. They are the best evidence we have so far,' he said earnestly. 'I am now going to get into the *Sanctum Sanctorum*,' the Doctor announced, seizing the telephone.

Bruce looked up in alarm. But before he could protest, the Doctor had assumed his Salamander voice and was giving orders for an escort to be sent to the

Behaviour Analysis Unit. 'I am releasing the two young prisoners from custody. They are to be conducted out of the Centre and freed immediately,' he rapped into the intercom.

Jamie and Victoria began to protest at having to desert their friend just as the real action was about to begin. But the Doctor was adamant.

Realising that it was too late to argue, Bruce stirred himself into action. 'Don't worry, McCrimmon, you still have a vital part to play,' he assured the angry young Scot, 'you and Miss Waterfield. Once you're out of here, get to a public telephone in Kanowa. Dial 007 and ask for Forester—he's my deputy. Tell him where I am and then just say *Redhead*. You understand? *Redhead*. It's our emergency codeword,' he explained.

The Doctor clicked his tongue impatiently. 'Bruce, you must go with Jamie and Victoria to ensure that they get out safely. Find them some transport to Melville.'

'What are *you* going to do?' Bruce demanded.

Pretending not to have heard, the Doctor fussed over his two young friends. 'You find your way back to the TARDIS and I'll meet you there. Jamie started to protest again. 'Just wait there until I come,' the Doctor ordered firmly.

At that moment the intercom buzzed. Forestalling Bruce, the Doctor seized it and answered in his Salamander voice. He listened in silent concentration for several seconds while the others looked on uneasily. 'No. Let him think he is undetected,' he snapped at last. 'I want to discover exactly what he is up to. Do not intercept him until I order it.' The Doctor replaced the receiver and turned to Donald Bruce. 'We have a visitor Bruce,' he announced dramatically. 'Time for you all to be going!'

9

Unexpected Evidence

Only minutes after leaving Swann lying in the cave, Astrid came across the capsule still parked in the shaft a few hundred metres down the tunnel. Once she had discovered the electronic key, carelessly left in its socket by Salamander, it only took her a few seconds to learn how to operate the capsule. When it whispered to a halt at the bottom of the shaft, she stepped out into the soft greenish glow of the underground Control Suite. She gazed down in astonishment at the scene in the cavernous laboratory. The white-overalled technicians were sitting hunched over plastic trays, eating and drinking from polythene food packs. They ate mechanically, without speaking or looking up. Astrid was appalled at the waxy pallor of their skin.

Fascinated, she moved over to the heavy shutter set into the end wall of the chamber and operated the touch-buttons. It slid smoothly aside and Astrid stepped out onto the metal landing at the top of the staircase in the corner of the laboratory. Suddenly someone spotted her. The technicians instantly vanished among the equipment like insects. Puzzled, she stood there, staring down at the humming, flickering instruments and the silently spinning computer discs.

'I have come to help you ... I have come to free you all ... to take you back to the surface,' she cried, spreading her arms out towards the invisible throng.

There was a brief silence. Then a plastic tray sliced through the air past Astrid's head and bounced clattering down the steps. She ventured down a step or two, her heart thudding and her mouth suddenly dry. 'Please don't be afraid. I want to help you,' she called out in a wavering voice. Immediately a hail of trays, cutlery and beakers came at her from all directions and she retreated back up the stairs again.

Colin Redmayne stood up in the centre of the cavern. 'Fools. You fools,' he cried, starting to walk towards the steps. 'It's a girl ... a human being ... from up there.'

Mary Smith appeared from behind her computer console. 'Colin, the radiation,' she warned him. But he walked on regardless.

A thick wooden batten from a packing case hurtled across the laboratory and struck Astrid viciously on the forehead. She stumbled and fell to the bottom of the stairs where she lay motionless. 'Please help me,' she gasped, her eyes glazed and her speech slurred.

'You are contaminated,' Colin said helplessly. Astrid stared up at him. 'You are from the surface,' he went on, 'therefore we must decontaminate you.'

The stranger shook her head slowly and pulled herself to her feet. She lurched a few steps towards Colin and he backed away from her.

Mary had moved hesitantly to Colin's side. 'Did you meet Salamander and Swann?' she asked nervously.

Astrid stared through her, searching her memory and fighting the blinding pain in her head. 'I think it was Swann,' she murmured, her voice seeming to come from a great distance. 'He sent me here. Swann is dead.'

A gasp of horror rose from the huddled technicians. It was followed by wave upon wave of helpless whispers.

In a faltering voice Astrid tried to explain that there was no lethal radiation on the surface, that Salamander had killed Swann and that he had been keeping them all prisoner underground for years. 'Salamander has been using you as slaves ... to carry out his plans for world domination ...'

There was a stunned silence.

'It's a lie. It can't be true! All this time down here, for *nothing*!' Colin Redmayne yelled, his eyes staring into empty space, as if he were in a trance. Some of the shelterers burst into tears, others stood motionless as if turned to stone.

Astrid clung to the stair rail fighting to stay conscious. 'Please, you must believe me,' she gasped.

Scurrying nimbly from doorway to doorway along the anonymous corridor, Giles Kent approached the Sanctum doors at the far end. He could scarcely believe his luck at having penetrated so far into the Research Centre without being challenged. His once smart clothes were now covered in dust and were ripped in several places as a result of his struggle to get through the labyrinth of narrow tunnels leading from the ravine into the disused buildings on the edge of the Centre compound.

Kent glanced cautiously around before moving across to the panel beside the heavy sealed doors of the Sanctum. For a moment he thought he detected a movement in one of the doorways. Rubbing his smarting eyes, he drew a small electronic key out of his shoe and with mounting excitement inserted it into the socket set in the panel. After a few seconds the Sanctum doors slid noiselessly open.

He approached the console in the centre of the Sanctum like a monarch returning to his throne. He did not see the small, neat figure slip through the doors behind him just an instant before they whispered shut, and when he turned to survey the room he seemed to be alone.

Like a child with some elaborate new toy, Kent sat himself in the plush swivel chair and became engrossed in trying out various combinations of touch-buttons on the console. Eventually the words *Locks Engaged* flashed up on the display in front of him.

'I am accustomed to visitors knocking before they enter, Mr Kent.' Salamander's acid voice cut through the humming stillness so unexpectedly that Kent froze for a moment, his hands raised over the console like an immobilised puppet's.

The Doctor emerged from behind a computer cabinet, his hand held out in greeting. 'A pleasure indeed, Mr Kent, but how did you get in here?' he asked, with a quizzical smile.

Giles rose slowly to his feet, trying desperately hard to master his astonishment. 'Oh, I still have a key,' he shrugged, attempting as sly grin. 'You forgot to take it away from me when I became a bad boy. I've been looking forward to this meeting, Salamander. It's been a long time.' Try as he would to be cool and impassive, Giles could not stop himself from betraying his tense excitement. 'I'm not alone this time, Salamander. I have some people in here with me and between us we're going to put an end to your Napoleonic fantasy,' he cried.

'You always were a tiresome little man, Kent,' the Doctor replied languidly, turning and walking away.

Stung by this typical insult, Giles moved round the

console with a mean glint in his eyes. 'And I'm going to be more tiresome than ever now,' he spat. 'Your biggest mistake was not killing me when you had the chance.'

The Doctor whipped round, stopping Kent in his tracks. 'So. Now you intend to kill *me* !' he retorted, his lips curling back and exposing his perfect teeth. 'And how do you imagine you will all manage without me? You seem to forget that my genius has given the world expectations of a new and glorious future,' he proclaimed. 'They must be fulfilled. And now the world is beginning to recognise its true Leader!'

Kent gave a scornful laugh. 'Well, the world's going to do without you from now on,' he cried. 'Who needs you now? The Sunstore operates by itself. Everything's automated. Everything's on tape.' He gestured at the racks of cassettes and data discs lining the Sanctum. 'You've been a bit too much of a genius Salamander; you've made yourself redundant, sport.'

As soon as he had escorted Jamie and Victoria safely out of the Research Centre, Donald Bruce had made straight for the Sanctum. He was now standing in the corridor outside the firmly sealed doors, watching the pale and tight-lipped Theodore Benik supervising a maintenance crew attempting to free the electrolocks. The panel beside the heavy doors had been opened and a thick bundle of tangled circuitry was hanging out of the wall.

Benik had been deep in thought. 'The locks appear to be still secured from inside. It doesn't make sense,' he muttered at last.

The chief technician looked up from the micro-circuit wafer he had been examining. 'I can't trace any fault at all, sir,' he told Benik. 'There's no way of by-passing the system. If you want to get in there, we'll have to burn our way in.'

One of the maintenance crew finished wiring an audio speaker into a section of the bundle of wires hanging out of the panel. When it was connected, the man looked inquiringly at the Deputy Director. Benik hesitated for several seconds. He knew that he was about to break one of the most sacred regulations of Salamander's organisation. Finally he gave a curt nod. The technician pressed a switch and the small speaker buzzed into life:

'... and even that crazy earthquake machine down there can be worked by those poor blind robots of yours,' Giles Kent could be heard sneering. 'All they need is feeding and watering.'

Benik jerked round to stare incredulously at Bruce. 'That's Giles Kent's voice!' he exclaimed. 'Kent's in there with the Leader. Giles Kent's in the Sanctum.' He snatched the speaker and put it to his ear, trying to distinguish the words of Salamander's murmured reply.

Donald Bruce did not need to hear any more. He ordered the chief technician to fetch a laser torch and to start cutting into the Sanctum doors.

As the technician ran off, Benik turned to Bruce with a dangerous laugh. 'You'll never cut through there!' he cried. 'It's an alloy: Salamandrium. It's impenetrable.'

'Well, you aren't!' Bruce snapped, reaching into Benik's tunic with a sudden deft movement and seizing the small pistol concealed there. He thrust the short barrel brutally into Benik's scrawny ribcage. 'So let's just wait and see, shall we?'

They heard Salamander's voice purring with triumph.

'So you see, Mr Kent, you are trapped. I have you completely at my mercy.'

Kent gave a weird, manic laugh which echoed eerily down the long corridor. 'You forget, Salamander. I know the back door, don't I?'

Without taking his eyes off Benik's perspiring face for an instant, Donald Bruce listened intently to the bizarre conversation coming out of the dangling speaker, desperately trying to visualise what was going on only a few metres away behind the impregnable doors.

Inside the Sanctum the Doctor was watching Giles Kent very carefully. He knew that he was on the brink of discovering all the evidence he needed against Salamander and also the truth about the wily Australian facing him.

'The back door, Giles?' he said quietly, smiling as if he and Kent were sharing a private joke or playing some game.

Kent laughed again, even more strangely than before. 'I've been in this room too many times to have forgotten where it leads.' He went to the console and quickly operated a sequence of touch-buttons before inserting his electronic key into the capsule system panel.

The Doctor's face remained expressionless as he watched the section of wall behind Giles Kent swing silently open, revealing the narrow, empty shaft beyond.

'Presto! Your little bolt-hole,' Kent cried, without turning round. He spread out his arms like a magician performing a sensational trick. 'And halfway down—the old mine-workings in the hillside, primed with

114

enough explosive to seal you up for ever should I care to light the …'

Kent had turned round. He saw that the capsule was not in position where it should be if Salamander was in the Sanctum. He swung wildly back to face the Doctor, his mouth hanging open and his eyes suddenly seeming to lose their colour. His hands gripped the edge of the console as if they were about to tear it apart.

Dropping all his Salamander mannerisms and reverting to his normal voice, the Doctor leaned across the console. 'How very interesting, Mr Kent. Why didn't you tell me all this before?' he exclaimed.

Kent's veined temples began to bulge again as he stared dumbfounded at the Doctor. 'It can't be … the Doctor … you …' he stuttered, blinking the sweat out of his eyes.

'And there's another surprise for you, Mr Kent!' the Doctor cried, pointing towards the shaft.

As Giles spun round, the capsule glided up and came to rest in the shaft behind him. Crammed inside were Astrid, Mary and Colin. The transparent shield whirred open and they all stepped out.

'Giles Kent!' Colin exclaimed. 'We thought you were dead.'

'It's *him*. He's the one who took us all down there!' Mary cried.

The Doctor watched intently as Astrid took a few steps towards her associate. 'I've realised the truth now, Giles You and Salamander were in this together right from the very beginning,' she said. Kent stood there in stunned silence while she turned to the Doctor. 'Giles built a so-called atomic shelter underneath here five years ago,' Astrid explained. 'He took a selected group of people down there as guinea pigs for a series of bogus endurance tests. Then Salamander appeared and told them that war had broken out between the Zones. Those people have been down there ever since.'

'A colony of subterranean slaves,' the Doctor exclaimed, eventually rousing himself from his reverie. 'Salamander needed a team to build and operate the ultimate secret weapon with which he could terrorise the world: a machine to create sham natural disasters and kill and injure innocent people.'

'And to fool the world!' Giles shouted defiantly at them. 'We fooled you all.'

The Doctor shook his head and smiled. 'Not quite, Mr Kent. You didn't fool me. I soon realised that you did not merely wish to expose Salamander, but that you wanted to take his place, using me as your stooge.'

With a sudden jerk of his wiry body, Giles snatched the electrokey out of the console and threw himself backwards into the capsule. 'And I will take his place. I will!' he shrieked triumphantly, waving the vital electrokey in their faces. 'No one can stop me now.'

Colin and Astrid rushed forward, but they were too late to prevent the shield closing. Safe behind the plastic glass, Kent laughed at them with manic derision, taunting them by holding up his own key and pointing to the one still inserted in the capsule's control panel. Mouthing insults, he operated the mechanism and the capsule slid smoothly downwards out of sight.

At once the Doctor strode to the console and stood frowning at the array of instruments. 'We must get out of here as fast as possible,' he told the others, who were standing looking helplessly at one another in front of the gaping shaft. 'If we don't, that madman might blow us all to pieces.' The Doctor stopped and glanced up at the Sanctum doors, sniffing the air and wrinkling his nose suspiciously. Then he hurried over and carefully put his hand near the hairline gap between the two sealed shutters. 'It's hot!' he cried, jumping back in alarm. 'Very hot.' He turned and faced the others with a broad grin. 'Somebody must be trying to cut their way in.'

Outside in the smoke-filled corridor Donald Bruce had been listening in grim-faced astonishment to the events taking place in the Sanctum and being relayed through the speaker. At the back of his mind lurked the constant fear that Jamie and Victoria had failed to contact his Deputy, Forester, and that Operation Redhead had therefore not been triggered. He knew that he was hopelessly outnumbered by Benik's personnel and that the confusion over Salamander's whereabouts and over the jamming of the Sanctum doors would not provide him with cover for much longer. Now he knew that Kent was threatening to detonate some of the installations, he was desperate to get the Doctor and the others out of the Sanctum.

All at once Bruce was overtaken by a fit of convulsive coughing. Instantly Benik twisted the pistol out of the Security Commissioner's hand and began to back away down the corridor.

'I've wanted to do this for a long time, Bruce,' he croaked, slipping the safety catch. Bruce peered through the thick haze, trying to clear his vision and preparing himself for a desperate attempt to dodge the imminent hail of bullets.

Suddenly the far end of the corridor filled with running, shouting WZO police officers. Panicking, Benik threw away his advantage and swung round to find himself confronted by a dozen levelled rifles. All the fight instantly left his tensed body and lowering his pistol, he allowed himself to be disarmed by a tall, visored figure.

'Forester, not a moment too soon. What kept you?' Bruce exclaimed, still choking from the smoke. 'I want all Research Centre personnel detained immediately, including Salamander himself, as soon as he is located. And you can start with this miserable little worm.'

As Benik was led away, the Doctor's voice suddenly came blasting out of the speaker connected into the circuitry beside the Sanctum doors. 'If that's you out there, Bruce, we have very little time,' the Doctor yelled, trying to make himself heard through the thick doors and completely unaware that he was more than audible outside. 'Unless you can get through in the next five minutes you had better evacuate the building. No sense in us all going up in smoke.'

Donald Bruce stared at the hissing beam of the laser torch through the billowing fumes. 'Come on. Come on,' he muttered anxiously. 'We must get them out of there.'

10

The Doctor Not Himself

When the capsule reached the level of the sloping tunnel, it ground to a shuddering halt. Uttering a string of vicious oaths, Kent opened the shield and stepped cautiously out into the dimly lit tunnel. As he began to examine the edges of the capsule and the shaft for some fault or obstruction, he heard a sudden movement behind him. Before he could turn round, an arm was flung round his neck and he was hurled sideways. Astrid's pistol flew out of his tunic and slithered away down the loose scree littering the tunnel floor.

A dark, compact figure sprang forward and grabbed it. Giles Kent found himself face to face with Salamander.

'You always were such a fool, Kent,' Salamander laughed, his eyes flashing with cruel amusement. 'You have not changed at all, amigo.'

'We're both finished!' Kent yelled at him, his voice ringing along the tunnels. 'They know up there. They know.'

Salamander advanced slowly towards him, a mask of a smile settling over his face. The white of his eyes and his teeth seemed to glow in the half-light. 'Really? And so what do you propose, Kent?' he mocked disbelievingly. 'Burying our differences? Forming a new alliance?'

Giles backed slowly up the tunnel. 'We can bury the evidence,' he pleaded. 'We planned for this, you and me.'

Salamander shook his head emphatically. 'Years ago I realised I did not need you, Kent,' he snarled, quickening his step so that Giles was forced to scramble clumsily backwards.

Salamander fired point-blank. Kent was hit in the chest and he fell to his knees at Salamander's feet. Salamander kicked him aside and walked away down the tunnel to the shaft.

Reaching underneath the capsule he removed the small wedge of flint he had earlier inserted in one of the grooved tracks in the shaft in order to disable it. Then he stepped in, closed the shield, and descended into the earth.

Clutching his shattered chest in agony, Giles Kent started to crawl up the tunnel. Eventually he managed to drag himself to his feet and to stagger up the relentless slope towards the ruined building where the supplies elevator shaft came out on the surface.

When the radiation hazard buzzer sounded in the cavernous chamber, the crowd of eagerly talking shelterers assembled round the staircase to the Control Suite turned and stared at the elevator hatch. They instantly fell silent at the sight of the bloodstained figure kneeling behind the glass panel and hammering on it. The man's face was hideously contorted as he uttered desperate, inaudible cries, his twisted features bathed in the pink glow of the 'decontamination process' which Astrid had exposed as a fake.

At first no one moved. Then one of the technicians operated the hatch mechanism and retreated quickly to join the crowd of shocked and fascinated onlookers. Giles Kent rolled out of the hatchway and staggered towards the staircase. As he began to drag himself up the metal steps someone gave a shout of angry recognition.

'It's Kent, Giles Kent, the collaborator!'

Dribbling streams of blood and shivering feverishly, Kent reached the door to the Control Suite. It was shut. Painfully slowly he fumbled for his own electrokey and then inserted it in the panel. The shutter opened and he stumbled into the Suite, making straight for the Console.

Salamander was standing by the capsule shaft, watching him with cynical amusement. 'I told you there was no escape, amigo,' he sneered.

With a final effort, Kent tottered forward and collapsed over the instruments. 'I'll damn well take you with me then,' he gasped, frantically jabbing the electrokey into a sequence of small sockets outlined in red.

Salamander sprang at him with a shriek of warning, but he was too late. There was a series of massive explosions deep in the underground installations. Shock waves buffeted the Control Suite and the laboratory for several seconds. Then the console started to disintegrate, throwing showers of sparking debris and dense jets of smoke in all directions. Kent's spread-eagled body was engulfed in searing flames and the chamber began to blister and melt around the defiant figure of Salamander.

In the Sanctum the Doctor and the others were thrown violently about as the force of the underground explosions roared up the capsule shaft. The console erupted in a spectacular firework display of blazing circuitry and the Sanctum doors were released. The

121

technicians outside forced the heavy shutters apart and Donald Bruce came lumbering anxiously into the Sanctum.

'Out of here before the whole plant goes up!' he urged, helping the Doctor back onto his feet while his officers shepherded Colin and Mary to safety. But Astrid held back, hovering by the smoke-filled shaft. 'Those people down there in the shelter!' she protested.

'What people?' Bruce demanded, still confused and anxious to take command of the situation.

The Doctor forced back a fit of coughing and turned Astrid to face him. 'They have almost certainly perished, my dear,' he murmured. 'I am so sorry.'

'But I promised. I promised Swann I would set them all free,' she cried, her face filled with anguish. 'I must find out if any are still alive. We can't just leave them down there now. I'm sure there are ways through from the ravine. We can at least try.' Despite Bruce's protests that the tunnels would have been destroyed, Astrid refused to move until he agreed to detail some of his men to attempt a breakthrough.

'Very well. You can have ten men for twenty-four hours,' he muttered, coughing and rubbing his watering eyes. 'And I'll come with you.'

Astrid nearly hugged the shambling figure as they hurried out of the Sanctum.

An hour later Donald Bruce and Astrid were standing in the Research Centre compound, shading their eyes as they watched the sleek white WZO helicopter rise into the spectacular evening sky. As it banked and flew away in the direction of Melville, Bruce turned to Astrid with a frown. 'Strange, isn't it? We never really found out who he was.'

122

They hurried back into the Administration Block where Bruce's deputy was organising the takeover of the Research Centre by the WZO authorities. As they entered the building, Forester came up to Bruce.

'We are in complete control now, Commissioner,' he reported. 'Benik is on his way to Geneva under full escort.' Bruce nodded his approval. 'Oh, and the Doctor sent his compliments to you. He flew out half an hour ago,' Forester added, turning away to supervise the confiscation of tapes and cassettes from the Sanctum.

Bruce gripped Forester's arm and swung him round again. 'What are you talking about? I've just this minute seen him off!' he exclaimed.

Forester returned Bruce's disbelieving look. Then his face went very, very pale . . .

Jamie had been sitting on the sand outside the TARDIS, watching a glorious sunset over the sea and wondering anxiously about the Doctor. For some time Victoria had been fast asleep in the big armchair inside the silent police box. Jamie was on the brink of nodding off himself when the sound of a distant motor brought him scrambling to his feet. He watched a tiny speck come whirring over the bay. It rapidly took shape as a small white helicopter which flew swiftly overhead and then turned sharply before hovering and finally settling on the beach close to the water's edge.

'It's himself. The Doctor's back,' he cried, thumping the side of the TARDIS to waken Victoria before setting off down the beach, eyeing the strange machine a little apprehensively.

The familiar figure clambered out of the cockpit, ducked under the slowing rotor blades and began walking unsteadily up the beach towards him.

'Och, we thought ye were never coming, Doctor!' Jamie shouted, waving happily. As the figure drew nearer, he saw that the Doctor's clothes were torn and covered in dust, and that every few metres he stumbled groggily. 'You're in a fine mess,' Jamie exclaimed. 'Whatever happened to you? I told you he'd be back before dark,' Jamie cried, following the Doctor into the TARDIS.

Victoria rubbed the sleep from her eyes and then sat bolt upright in the armchair, staring at the Doctor in dismay. 'I *knew* we should never have left you,' she said.

The Doctor ignored her and went straight over to the control column in the centre of the chamber. He gazed around him as if he could hardly believe how roomy it was. He leaned over the controls, glassy-eyed and slightly trembling.

Jamie went over to him. 'Are you all right, Doctor?' he asked anxiously. 'You look terrible.'

The Doctor seemed to be breathing with great difficulty. He raised both hands and gestured helplessly at the mass of instruments, levers, switches, gauges and indicator lights littering the circular structure which resembled something out of an amusement arcade.

'You want to make a start, Doctor?' Victoria suggested, with a puzzled glance at Jamie.

The Doctor nodded vigorously. He gestured to Jamie and then back to the controls, as if inviting the young Highlander to take command. Jamie retreated round the console in confusion.

Victoria joined Jamie on the opposite side of the console. 'But, Doctor, you said we were never to touch anything ... any of the machinery,' she murmured.

'That's quite right, Victoria,' said a familiar voice.

The figure opposite them spun round to face the newcomer silhouetted against the sunset in the open doorway. Jamie and Victoria looked up in astonishment.

The Doctor was standing there, not quite so ragged and dusty, contemplating Salamander with a grim smile.

'So. We meet at last. I had a feeling this would happen eventually,' the Doctor said drily, advancing a few paces.

Salamander was backed up hard against the console, gripping the edge of the panelling with white-knuckled hands. 'Buenas tardes,' he replied after a moment's silence. 'You have impersonated me so brilliantly, Doctor, that I just had to return the compliment.'

The Doctor stepped a little closer to Salamander. 'I regret that I must ask you to leave now,' he said quietly. 'We have to be on our way.' Salamander did not move. 'Oh, and I took the liberty of pouring a couple of shoes full of seawater into your fuel tank out there,' the Doctor added with a cheeky grin. 'But don't worry. Bruce won't take long to find you.'

With a strange hissing murmur Salamander began to speak. 'Such a needless waste, Doctor. Two men of such genius as we two. What glorious things we could achieve together, you and I. What a future we could give to the world.'

Jamie had noticed Salamander's hands moving stealthily towards the controls behind him as he spoke. Suddenly he sprang forward, pinning Salamander's arms to his sides. Salamander rolled abruptly sideways, taking Jamie with him as he spread-eagled himself over the console.

'Hold on!' the Doctor yelled, grabbing Victoria's arm with one hand and the edge of the console with the other as the TARDIS began to shudder and an unearthly grinding noise began to fill the blood-red air around

125

them. Lights flickered madly all round the console and the door banged wildly to and fro as the police box began to roll and spin dizzily. Jamie let go of Salamander and threw himself towards the massive armchair, grabbing a leg and clinging on for dear life.

Like some crazy merry-go-round, the TARDIS oscillated faster and faster. A maelstrom of blackness and roaring and of hurricane winds swirled them helplessly around. The Doctor was shouting instructions at the top of his voice, but nobody could hear what he was trying to say. The air itself seemed to be vibrating like a plucked string and it became impossible to breathe properly as everybody's lungs rapidly inflated and deflated in time with the pulsations of everything around them. Victoria felt as though she were engulfed in some unspeakable nightmare. When she twisted her head round to look at the figure whose hand she was desperately clutching, she seemed to see only the monstrous Salamander, his teeth bared and his eyes burning with crazed delight. And when she looked the other way across at the maddened creature grappling frenziedly with the console, she seemed to see the Doctor, deliberately throwing the TARDIS out of control and steering them all into an endless limbo where Time and Space were inextricably entwined, trapping them for ever.

Suddenly the console began to buck and rear up like an unbroken horse. Salamander lost his grip on the controls and was flung high into the air. For a moment he hung over them all like an enormous bird of prey, then his body seemed to be pulled in all directions at once as if it were made of rubber. It was swept up in an invisible vortex which drew it relentlessly towards the gaping doorway. Above the din there was a sudden prolonged hissing noise, and Salamander was sucked out into the empty roaring blackness where he instantly disintegrated in the middle of nowhere ...

Victoria felt the Doctor's grip tighten around her wrist as he dragged himself painfully closer to the shuddering controls. Jamie too had managed to grab hold of a stanchion supporting the console. He let go of the massive armchair and it immediately started careering crazily around the TARDIS with a life of its own.

The Doctor was no longer shouting. With his forehead pressed against the console he seemed to be murmuring gentle, reassuring words to his beloved apparatus, trying to calm it enough to give him time to reach the vital stabilisers and thus regain control. His two young friends were suddenly filled with hope. Salamander really did seem to have disappeared for ever, and they knew they could trust the Doctor. He had never let them down. Now they willed him to succeed as his outstretched hand finally closed round the stabiliser lever and gradually but firmly adjusted the setting.

After what seemed an eternity, the TARDIS at last began to respond, and all at once Jamie and Victoria found themselves laughing and cheering with relief. Glancing at the Doctor, they saw that familiar look of intense and insatiable curiosity come over his face as the uproar subsided and the police box gradually stopped shaking so violently.

They knew that they were about to materialise yet again in some unknown corner of the Universe. Although they did not yet know where it would be, they were certain that it would not be a dull place. And in the end, that was all that really mattered ...